# REQUIEM OF MAGIC

# REQUIEM OF MAGIC
## THE LEIRA CHRONICLES™ BOOK 13

MARTHA CARR
MICHAEL ANDERLE

DISRUPTIVE IMAGINATION

DON'T MISS OUR NEW RELEASES

Join the LMBPN email list to be notified of new releases and special promotions (which happen often) by following this link:

http://lmbpn.com/email/

This book is a work of fiction. All of the characters, organizations, and events portrayed in this novel are either products of the author's imagination or are used fictitiously. Sometimes both.

Copyright © 2024 Martha Carr and Michael T. Anderle
Cover Art by Jake @ J Caleb Design
http://jcalebdesign.com / jcalebdesign@gmail.com
Cover copyright © LMBPN Publishing

LMBPN Publishing supports the right to free expression and the value of copyright. The purpose of copyright is to encourage writers and artists to produce the creative works that enrich our culture.

The distribution of this book without permission is a theft of the author's intellectual property. If you would like permission to use material from the book (other than for review purposes), please contact support@lmbpn.com. Thank you for your support of the author's rights.

LMBPN Publishing
2375 E. Tropicana Avenue, Suite 8-305
Las Vegas, Nevada 89119 USA

Version 1.00, January 2024
eBook ISBN: 979-8-88878-650-5
Print ISBN: 979-8-88878-770-0

The Oriceran Universe (and what happens within / characters / situations / worlds) are Copyright (c) 2017-2024 by Martha Carr and LMBPN Publishing.

THE REQUIEM OF MAGIC TEAM

**Thanks to the JIT Readers**

Veronica Stephan-Miller
Zacc Pelter
Diane L. Smith
Dorothy Lloyd
Jan Hunnicutt

# CHAPTER ONE

The four Witches trailed each other down the midway at the Texas State Fair stumbling past the fifty-five-foot papier mâché cowboy, Big Tex, that was set up in the middle of the fairgrounds. They picked up speed by the rows of booths selling Texas Fried Frito Pie or large turkey legs or deep-fried anything. Their destination was still a few hundred yards away and their pursuers were not far behind. The Witches needed to keep it that way. A plan was in motion.

"Keep going," snarled Lois over her shoulder at the other two Witches without really looking back. The fourth Witch, Patsy was already lingering, standing in line at the Fletcher's booth waiting for a corn dog. It was a part of a carefully timed contrivance to pull the magicals hunting them toward the back of the fair. Make them think they had a chance.

Finally, Patsy caught up by the games of chance, closer to their rendezvous point. The greasy smell of cornbread and hot dog floated in the air around her.

"This way ladies!" The two Witches in the middle ignored the carneys' loud chants. Lois gave a quick nod of recognition but kept moving. "Your lucky day has arrived!" bellowed the skinny whip of a man. His greying mustache covered his mouth, the drooping sides hanging down past his chin. He was standing in a spacious booth with water guns evenly spaced out, attached to a wooden counter by a long hose. He turned his back to them and waved his arms, drawing the attention toward himself. "Who's next? Who would like to win a stuffed elephant? How about you, sir?"

The women passed by three more booths, unnoticed by the other barkers who had sized them up and already decided they weren't the sort to stop and play. The Witches were wearing what passed for a disguise at a state fair. Variations of waist-high pedal pushers and comfortable shoes with an oversized t-shirt and a large faux leather purse. No one gave them a second look.

"Slow down, will you? I almost dropped my corny dog." Patsy chomped down hard on the top of the corn dog on a stick, taking a quick glance over her shoulder at the midway entrance behind her.

Lois clenched her fist and let the fingers roll back out slowly in a wave, releasing a volley of tiny gold fireballs that dropped to the ground, gliding backward quickly till they were under Patsy's feet. *Crack! Sizzle!*

Patsy swallowed hard, gulping and hopping on one foot and then the other, grumbling as she took another bite. "Son of a leather toadstool! A little harsh," she muttered.

"Focus," snapped Lois, tucking her hand into her pocket. The tips of her fingers were still tingling. "They're not far behind. Hurry. We're only getting one chance at this. If we blow this, the war against the Silver Griffins goes on for years. Besides, that's your third corny dog. Give it a rest."

Patsy tap-tapped the outline of her wand hidden deep in her pants pocket. "Not often you get this nervous. It's gonna be okay. You'll be home in time for dinner with Earl. Well, home somewhere."

Lois looked back at her old friend who shrugged, but she quickly turned around, careful not to draw attention. Not yet. "One chance, Patsy."

The Witch in the front of the group ducked between two of the booths that were shaded by royal blue awnings. The other three fell in line, moving rapidly past low plastic pools on a painted wooden platform, filled with bright yellow toy ducks. The jointee in the booth gave a slight nod as they moved down the side. Another ally in plain sight. He turned back to the crowd of excited children and anxious parents. "Ten tries for two dollars! Who's up for a challenge?"

The Witches finally became hidden from view by the large plush toys strategically hanging on the sides of the booth. Over-sized crayons, elephants and pink flamingos were smashed together creating a furry curtain. Patsy swallowed the rest of her corny dog, still moving, acutely aware of the time and heading toward the destination. The Witch right in front of her stumbled, almost falling to her knees but Patsy grasped her shoulders and pulled her upright. "I'm freakishly strong," she whispered, smiling at the Silver Griffin agent. "Come on, we can do this."

The jointee working the booth scanned the area over the heads of the group gathered in front of him, looking back toward the tower building. He spotted the tall Light Elf first, making his way toward his booth. The Elf was on the Silver Griffins *most wanted list*, back when they still had one. "There we go, come on," the carnival worker growled under his breath, startling a young mother. He quickly smiled and patted the tow-headed child in front of her with his meaty palm. "Tell you what, just because, how about we let you try the first round for free?"

He looked back up again, watching two more Light Elves trailing the first one, winding through the crowd and bumping into others along the midway. Behind them were a pair of gnomes, matching tattoos covering opposite sides of their faces. "Marcus brothers," muttered the jointer. "Nothing but the best trash has come out to play." He turned his back and breathed into his cupped hands, spinning around in time to release a stream of clear bubbles, delighting the children. The bubbles floated on the breeze, rising overhead, making a sudden turn toward Lois and the other Witches, picking up speed till they were right overhead.

*Pop, pop, pop! Six headed your way.*

The words floated down around Lois just as her hand reached for the side door of the horse barn. She hesitated, giving the pursuers a chance to gain ground. The old leader of the Silver Griffins stepped halfway over the threshold of the barn and reached inside her pocket, pulling out her wand. She pulled the other witches in, shoving them to the right and gave an uneasy smile to the former Fixer waiting in the shadows.

"Right this way, ladies," said Turner Underwood, doffing his bowler and tapping his cane hard against the soft dirt floor. "Patsy, you too," he said, firmly, even as Patsy pulled out her wand and turned to stand next to Lois.

"I'm afraid that's not how we do things around here, staged or not," said Patsy. "If this... if this goes another way, then I go out standing next to my friend."

"There's no time," yelled Lois, lifting her wand overhead and whipping out a long gold whip lined with razor-sharp tiny spikes. The whip found its mark, digging into the cheek of one of the Marcus brothers and leaving a jagged gash along the tattoo, erupting in blood. The gnome screamed out in pain and barreled forward, even as the Elves began tossing fireballs.

"You're cornered now, you old crone!" yelled a Light Elf.

"Very well," said Turner, raising the cane up in the air and circling it over the heads of the remaining Witches. "I will return shortly." The trio vanished in a flash of sparkling light leaving only Lois and Patsy framed in the doorway.

"Have you noticed that we spend a lot of time mixing a little fun with a lot of fireworks?" asked Patsy. "We really need to start a book club or take up gardening."

Lois let out a laugh and cracked the dangerous whip again wrapping it around the ankles of the closest Light Elf, tearing at the flesh and pulling him off his feet just as a fireball whizzed past her head, singeing her hair.

Patsy sniffed the air and looked at Lois' head. "That's gonna take a minute to grow back out." She flicked her wand in a neat square and blew in the center, sending out a pulse that landed neatly in the gut of the other Marcus brother, rolling him backward in a ball.

"Nicely done," said Lois.

A fireball hit the side of the barn catching it on fire, sending up screams from people nearby. The crowd turned and looked on in surprise and wonder at magic out in the open. Their reactions quickly turned to horror. The hidden magicals who were out with their families drew back, fleeing with the other fairgoers even as Lois and Patsy took a step back together into the burning barn.

Inside, the barn was empty, the main doors blocked to keep anyone from accidentally entering. The horses had already been moved out as well, getting ready for what was to come next.

"Now," said Lois quietly, taking her friend's hand and squeezing it tight. The two Witches raised their wands in unison, sending out a stream of fireballs, peppering the magical thugs and holding them in their positions.

The Elves and the Marcus Brothers stopped just short of the barn and formed a semi-circle as one of the Elves worked to quickly throw a magical ward around the perimeter, preventing anyone from being able to escape. Liam Marcus reared back his head and let out a satisfied howl, cut short by a fireball hitting his shoulder and catching his members-only jacket on fire. He slapped at the blue flames, yipping and snarling. "Motherfuckers, this is vintage! Enough. Set the whole thing on fire. Use the blue fucking flame!"

"We need a body to collect the bounty," yelled a Light Elf with a nose that had been broken more than once.

"Sam said he'd take proof of death. That doesn't necessarily mean a body. We'll give him a show that will leave no doubts," snarled Sean Marcus.

The Marcus Brothers spread their hands wide overhead, blue electrical sparks jumping from hand to hand, picked up by the Light Elves standing on either side, and rising till it formed a blue checkerboard curtain that slowly collapsed over the roof of the barn.

Patsy's eyes grew large, watching the light show and she pushed against the invisible wall trapping them in, her mouth opening wide. Lois pulled her back further into the darkness of the barn as Patsy kicked the door shut behind them.

"You were chewing the scenery there a bit," shouted Lois over the roar of the fire. The roof was becoming completely engulfed and the edges were beginning to collapse.

"They're a bunch of morons," said Patsy, her cheeks bright red from the heat. "Subtlety is wasted on them. You said they have to get the point."

*Crack*! A stretch of ceiling fell to the ground as Lois and Patsy ran for the far side of what remained of the barn.

"Turner is cutting things a little close." The ground under their feet rumbled and shook as the spell holding them in began to squeeze tighter and tighter, compressing the building. Patsy looked at Lois and opened her mouth to say something, but nothing came out and her face was turning a pale blue. Lois squeezed her eyes shut and willed herself to remain standing. "Come on, old girl. You can do it," she gasped.

In the center of the chaos a space emerged, and Turner appeared, beckoning to the two Witches. "Lois, he's here," nudged Patsy, barely getting out the words.

Turner pulled them close, raising his cane and

bellowing loud enough to be heard over the crackling fire. "If it's the last good thing we do!"

Lois's head felt like it was swimming, the thunder and heat from the fire giving way to a cool blackness just as the barn gave in and exploded into a thousand splinters and twisted metal beams. The sound was deafening but lasted only a moment before the darkness opened up and she found herself standing in the retired Fixer's library. The other two Witches were already there, patiently waiting.

Steam was pouring off Lois' body and her eyes were watering.

"I smell like I was in a deep fryer," said Patsy, letting out a relieved sigh, pulling a corny dog out of her pocket.

"The timing had to be perfect and at the very last possible moment," said Turner.

"Well done then." Lois took in a deep breath, letting it out slowly.

"They have ways to know if there were still magicals in the building or not. Any sooner and they would have known that you all escaped, and this was one big ruse."

"But it worked and at the state fair with people running for their lives." Patsy waved her hands in the air. "That should get some attention. Now we're all officially dead, right?" She tenderly touched a new hole in her sleeve where a spark had burned.

"Till further notice," said Turner.

"This should take some of the heat off the rest of the Silver Griffin agents out there. No one will think we can reorganize," said Lois. "All the big fish have been caught or killed." She rubbed her temples.

"The funeral should cement it for everyone. I'll make

the arrangements in Chicago." Turner took off his hat, resting it on the large polished wooden desk. He tilted his head to one side giving a wry chuckle. "A small affair, of course, under the circumstances. Magicals will not want to be gathered in a group. Not right now."

"Strange times ahead." Lois drew her mouth into a pinched straight line, her brows drawn together. "Usually, we are doing the hunting."

"Give it time," said Turner. "The Silver Griffins will rise again and perhaps with a few new twists to the story. Until then, let's be on our way. The next stop on your escape route is anxiously awaiting you." Turner picked up his hat and pressed it onto his head, tapping his cane and with a *whoosh*, the library was empty again.

---

Two days later Turner stood in the courtyard of St. James Cathedral next to the young rector, Reverend Gleason. There was already a cold chill in the air despite the early days of fall.

A body floated above the basin located just outside the entrance to the labyrinth. The stone pool was once again full of water from the rivers of Rodania. The only other mourners were General Anderson in his uniform, his medals neatly pinned in rows on his chest and Leira and Correk standing by his side, quietly waiting.

The general broke the silence leaning over to whisper to Leira. "Who exactly are we mourning? Unofficially."

Leira looked straight ahead at the statue of the Arpak, its arms outstretched. "An agent named Sadie Castro. She was ambushed near Cincinnati and died in Correk's arms. Sadie served in the Silver Griffins for over a hundred years and deserved a better ending."

Correk grimaced, letting out a troubled breath. "This will always be her resting place. Sadie represents all the agents we've lost these past few months."

The general looked up at the floating body. "A ringer for Lois. I'm going to go ahead and guess that's a little bit of magic."

"A temporary glamour. It will wear off over the next few days and Sadie will be remembered forever just as she was. Her last act of service is to stand in for Lois and help the Silver Griffins fight on." Leira took Correk's hand and leaned into his shoulder. "A peaceful oasis in the middle of chaos."

"Take it in," said Correk. "This may be our last moments before we go out there and try to figure out this new world where magic is out in the open."

Turner appeared behind them, leaning both hands heavily on the silver knob of his cane, his long, woolen coat buttoned to the top against the wind. "See me after the funeral, Leira. I have an idea that may help in the days ahead."

"Good, because this will stop," said Leira. "We'll make it so."

The rector cleared his throat and the small band turned to face the door that lead to the resting place of revered Witches and Wizards. Reverend Gleason began the Oriceran prayer and everyone bowed their heads in silence.

## CHAPTER TWO

Leira woke up in the small log cabin tucked at the base of the Coal Creek Canyon, not too far from Sedona, Arizona.

She was curled in a corner of the lumpy, king-sized bed with a faded patchwork quilt pulled up under her chin. She lifted her head enough to look at the old stove in the corner. "No fire. Hey, I don't suppose you could pile on a few logs. Hey--" She leaned a bare arm out just far enough to poke the curling troll sleeping in a tired-looking snake plant.

Yumfuck yawned and opened one eye. "What? Brrrrr." His little body shook and he rolled over, wiggling down deeper in the dirt. It wasn't long before he was snoring and kicking his feet.

"That's what I thought." Leira let out a sigh and reached behind her, smoothing over the empty space. She sat up, brushing her bangs out of her face and swung her legs toward the bare wooden floor before she could think about it. The cold shot up through her legs and she bit down, running the few feet across the room to the pile of wood next to the potbelly stove. "Almost there," she said through gritted teeth. "Make a pyramid and fuck the rest. No more fatwood, no kindling." She danced around on the balls of her feet, rubbing her arms. A snort of tiny laughter rose from the plant behind her. "I could always use an old deck of cards as filler."

"You wouldn't dare." The troll sat up and crawled to the edge of the plant, blinking and rubbing his face. "Use a fireball. Just a little one. Do it! Do it!" He stood up in the plant, dancing in a circle with his tiny paws over his head.

"They don't know I'm a magical. Fuck. Hell with it. I can see my breath." Leira's eyes began to glow as three small fireballs grew in her palm. She gently rolled them into the stove and watched as they caught fire. "That kind of fire won't go out easily." She shut the door on the stove and stood back, feeling the warmth spreading up her torso. Yumfuck threw a leg over the edge of the chipped green pot and dropped to the floor, scrambling over to Leira and crawling up the leg of her cotton pajama bottom. She plucked him off and lifted the furry troll to her shoulder.

He laid back against her hair and smiled. "Ahhhhh, aloha motherfuckers. This is living."

---

"Why aren't we using a portal?" The troll looked up at Leira from inside her shirt pocket. He was wearing a tiny flannel shirt Eireka had made him but still no pants. Too much chafing against the fur.

Leira was sitting behind the wheel of a cherry red

Subaru Forester, backing out of the gravel parking spot. Rocks spit out from the tires as she turned the car and slowly cruised past the large sign at the entrance. *Don Hoel's Cabins* was painted inside of a red heart and hanging on a wooden post. "Turner Underwood said, where we're going you can't portal into. Besides, we'd miss all the scenery if we zip by it." Leira patted the headrest of the other seat. "Get up where you can see out and watch the world go by. This is one of the most beautiful places on this planet and some say, has the most natural magic." Leira had been fighting the urge since she got there to let the magic flow through her. A couple of times her eyes had involuntarily started to glow, including while checking in and she had to quietly turn and look out the windows and think about baseball.

"Road trip! Where are the snacks?" Yumfuck looked crestfallen, searching the empty floorboards of the car.

"We'll stop and load up. I know the rules. Anything over an hour and outside of the county line gets the proper set of junk food. Let me get to a gas station and I'll buy one of everything."

The troll climbed out of Leira's pocket and onto her shoulder bounding over to the passenger side headrest and neatly landing with a loud, "Whoop!"

They wound their way out of the dense woods, the colorful, striated cliffs in the distance marking their way to Camp Verde, a couple of hours away, down the old state route, one-seventy-nine, the red rock highway. Yumfuck spent most of the ride standing on the edge of the door with his face pressed against the window, oohing and aahing at the red cliffs, interspersed with a song about snacks. "There'll be red vines, and jerky and icees and more," he trilled. Leira turned up the radio and gave a crooked smile, symbols creeping up her hands and slowly flipping over.

"This never happens on Oriceran," she muttered. "Was it about this place?" Energy was slowly swirling in the pit of her stomach, warming the nearby scar. Her ears had a mild buzz that occasionally crackled and sparked.

"Circle K! Circle K!" Yumfuck was balancing on one tiny paw, the claws dug into the upholstery, waving his arms and slapping the window. Leira pulled into the parking lot and parked at the far right end away from the other cars. She plucked the troll off the edge of the window, holding him in the palm of her hand where she could look him in the eye. "I'm the only one who goes in, deal?"

"Well..."

"No one goes in or only I go in," she said, restarting the car. "People know about magic now and they won't be so quick to assume you're a very clever mouse. How badly do you want snacks?"

The troll pressed his paws against his chest. "So very badly."

"I will keep my word and wait in the car badly? Or I will wait, lose my cool and risk it badly?"

Yumfuck blew out a large breath of air, his cheeks puffing out. "Somewhere in the middle."

"Alright then. Nesturnium."

Yumfuck gasped. "Low blow, after all we've been through."

"You don't know where we're going, or more importantly who we're going to see. We can't take any chances. I'll tell you what. I'll bury you in candy, Cheetos and fried anything I can find. Maybe they even have Dr. Pepper in these parts."

"Like I have a choice." The troll sat down heavily.

"True, but I'll do it anyway. After all we've been through, trust me. It will all make sense soon."

## CHAPTER THREE

Yumfuck was sleeping on his back atop a pile of trash on the floor of the car, his leg dangling just inside a Doritos bag. "Num, num, num," he said, smacking his lips.

"That must be some dream." Leira's heart was beating faster with every mile, the closer they got to their destination. She glanced over as they passed the sign, *The Castle of Montezuma*.

"Cliff dwellings of the Sinigua, next exit," she muttered. Her face was warm, and she glanced in the rearview mirror at her eyes. They were glowing a steady bright green. "That's new."

She reached over and dug her hand through her purse, keeping her eyes on the road. The Subaru's wheels crossed briefly into the next lane anyway, making the driver next to her pull hard to the left and lean on his horn. He shook his fist angrily at Leira till he saw her eyes, his mouth dropping open. A half-hearted middle finger curled back down.

"Found them." Her fingers curled around the sunglasses and she pulled them out, shaking them open, sliding them on her face. "Maybe we could have portaled most of the way here."

"What was that?" A drowsy troll stirred, licking the day-glow orange dust on his arm. "Mmmm, Cheetos dust." He closed his eyes and laid back.

"We're almost there, Yumfuck. A good time to pull your shit together." Leira tapped her fingers rhythmically on the steering wheel.

Yumfuck opened one eye and stared up at her. "Are we talking battle ready?" He attempted to sit up but was firmly stuck to a Sugar Daddy. "Houston, we have a problem." He tried rolling over, sharp teeth bared to bite his way out of it, but he was stuck.

Leira glanced down and gave him a crooked smile, making herself take a slow and measured breath. "Wow, done in by caramel on a stick. Finally found your Kryptonite. You gonna figure this out?"

"Give me a second. Son of a bitch!" Yumfuck tried rolling his feet over his head but only succeeded in sticking another paw to the warm caramel. He was curled up in a sticky, furry ball, his legs over his head. "A little help here," he squeaked, his tiny butt in the air.

"Hang on, trying to drive and rescue you." *And stay calm. What is with this energy?* Leira grabbed the empty Doritos bag and leaned down, doing her best to still be able to see the road. At the last second, she looked over and grabbed the troll, lifting him onto the seat. "This is a rental. Try not to completely do in the upholstery."

"Too late. Now I'm stuck to the seat." He grunted, wriggling his butt, but not getting anywhere. "Come on. A little magic over here."

Leira saw the exit and pulled off the highway, sensing the energy growing even more. "Of all the ridiculous things." She took a deep breath and let the energy seep in further, rolling down her arm to her fingertips, warming her skin. She put her hand over the troll, holding it there as he let out a satisfied trill. "Warm at last," he cooed. The caramel melted, bonding with the cloth seats as the troll wriggled free.

"That's gonna leave a stain."

"Maybe," said the troll, carefully biting his way through what remained of the candy.

Leira looked away, shaking her head. "Let go of everything," she whispered, repeating the advice Turner Underwood had given her when he handed over the directions. "Let the experience happen. No judgment, no thinking. The energy will carry me if I let it. Fight it and it'll fight back. No kidding." She took in another long breath.

Yumfuck looked up at her, caramel smeared across his face, making his fur stick out in points, ending in a candy-coated green mohawk on the top of his head. "Wait a minute. Where are we going?"

"Montezuma's Castle, I told you before we left." Leira followed the signs, turning and turning until she could see the cliff dwellings in the distance. *Getting close. Our second meeting.*

The troll lifted his nose and sniffed the air. "Who are we going to see? Who, who, who?" he sang, his eyes growing wider. "So much magic in the air. Energy is flowing everywhere. I can smell it." He smacked his lips together. "There are energy trails everywhere. Can you see them?"

Leira's brow furrowed and she looked back at the road in the direction of the cliff dwellings. In front of her were different colored streams of pulsating light weaving in and out of each other creating a mesmerizing quilt. The buzzing was picking up in her ears.

"There's only one being who can create trails like that." The troll scampered up to the headrest and leaped across to the dashboard, pressing his face against the windshield. "Ooooh, pretty. The seer is close by. You found Tess."

"How do you-- never mind. She was never lost. The old Fixer always knew where she was living."

"We're off to see the Wizard," sang Yumfuck.

"Yeah, it does feel like we're arriving in a weird version of Oz," said Leira, watching the dials in the car spit out rapidly changing numbers. "Where none of the usual rules apply."

"Well, weird's kind of our brand." The troll howled, arching his back as Leira watched the streams hesitate, shaking from side to side.

"I think it knows we're here."

---

Leira pulled the car into the empty gravel lot and parked at the far side toward the caverns, as instructed. She got out as a park ranger strode over, doffing his wide-brimmed hat. He took a moment to smooth down a stray curl of bright red hair. On his chest was a plastic name tag that read, '*Mike Mitchell*'. "Afternoon. We've been expecting you, Leira Berens."

"Where are all the tourists?"

"We close the place every year on certain dates when the magic is running particularly high. Did no one tell you? It's not an accident that you're here today. The veil between the living and the dead is particularly strong. Nothing can reach out from the World in Between until nightfall. Then this surge of magic will collide with the desire of everything trapped on the other side." He managed to make a smile look like a grimace. "Not to worry. We know how to keep everything tucked in. This has been happening for a thousand years. This weekend when the tourists come back through here the magic will be on a more tolerable level and the World in Between will be keeping its hands to itself, once again. You understand the rules?" The ranger nodded at the troll. "Does everyone understand the rules?"

"Don't disturb or remove any artifacts. Leave everything the way we found it and use no magic, so we leave no specific trail for anyone to follow."

"Thank you. Take your time on the hike. It's simple, a straight path, but not easy. The magic will push back at you. Even you. At times it will feel like you're climbing up a steep path and there will be a stretch where you will be, making it even harder. Hope you've been working out."

Leira bit her bottom lip. "Why does it matter if I use magic or not? There are hundreds of trails of magic that lead straight here already."

"Those make a specific pattern and are from the magic that surrounds the area. They don't start anywhere specific, and they don't end at any particular destination. No magical will guess it portends something else, particularly those we wish to keep out." He put his hat back on with a nod and turned to go, calling out over his shoulder. "Better get a move on. The magic grows stronger when the sun sets. It can be difficult to break through."

"And there's the whole World in Between leaking." Leira shifted her weight, looking down at her hiking boots, wondering if she should have brought running shoes.

He waved his hand. "I'll see you on your return. Enjoy your visit. You're a very lucky magical. Not many get an invitation. Not many at all."

Leira took in a deep breath and let it out slowly, willing her heart rate to slow down. "Come on, you're not walking into a battle. Get a grip." She set out with Yumfuck on her shoulder, gently pushing through a thick stand of saplings. *Next step. Follow the blue trails of light.*

"Follow, follow, follow, follow the very blue road," the troll sang quietly.

She ducked under branches, carefully stepping over boulders covered in lichen, following a sparkling azure blue stream of light for a mile as the canopy grew denser overhead, blocking out most of the light dappling the trail.

The troll stood on her shoulder, ducking down when a branch brushed just over his head, but staying unusually quiet for the last half mile. Every step of the way branches pushed back at them, once knocking Leira to the ground. She got back up, only to be pushed over again by the same tree. "I don't give up easily, or ever," she yelled, her voice echoing back to her.

"You're trying to start a fight with trees." Yumfuck leaned closer, holding on to her collar and patted the side of her face.

"Yeah, well, they started it."

"Boom, got 'em. Feel better?" The troll sat down on her shoulder, Leira still sitting on the ground. "You can do this, Leira. Fit yourself to your surroundings. Don't keep insisting they fit you."

Leira arched a brow and smiled. "Let the magic help me." She took a different tack and crawled just far enough to be out of reach of the tall pine tree and stood up, pushing through the next series of branches even as they scratched her face, and pulled at her jacket. "Don't resist," she whispered, slowly shutting her eyes and feeling her way further down the path. *Step. Step. Step.* Branches brushed against her, poking her in the arms and the chest but she was staying upright.

Finally, the trees bent back just enough for Leira and the troll to pass through more easily. Leira opened her eyes and felt her heart slowing down, at last. The space had opened onto a wide, dry riverbed that was kept hidden by the forest that had grown up around it. Barely any light reached the long stretch of dry earth that disappeared into the darkness. Only the blue light illuminated the area right around them, helping Leira see where it was safe to step and what to avoid.

"Help me," she said, as the light branched out, running down the embankment and filling the deepest parts of the barren ground. "Nothing is growing where the river used to be." She looked up at the trees. "These trees have been here for decades, at least, but nothing. Not even moss." Leira made her way easily down the bank and stepped into the middle. The scar on her belly burned as the blue light crept up her legs and surrounded her torso.

"Friend or foe?" asked the troll, ready to hop off Leira's shoulder and take his place by her side.

*Whoosh!*

As suddenly as it rose, the light slid back down and made a sharp left turn, traveling straight down the middle of the uneven ground. "Okay, that felt like an invitation." Leira picked her way across the dry riverbed, stepping over rocks and pottery shards. An iguana ran across a rock, glancing up at Leira, disappearing into a crevice. Her boots sunk an inch into the ground, and she struggled to lift each foot, still walking toward her destination. The cliff dwellings and the seer.

"Friend, for now. Better keep moving," said Leira. She looked down at her boots, expecting to see mud but was surprised at the red dust swirling around her feet, lost in the blue light. Each step was getting harder and her legs felt heavy and getting heavier.

"Mike did not oversell it. The magic is pushing back," said Leira, feeling the weight against her chest. Yumfuck was leaning in the direction of the caves, the energy holding him up even as he leaned out further.

Leira pulled out her phone to check the time. *Already eleven a.m. Still plenty of time till sundown. But no signal. No way to make a phone call or send an email.* She opened her hand, about to try and open a portal when she remembered the instructions. She closed her hand and kept trudging, her shirt damp from sweat, chilling her to the bone in the dark woods. She kept moving, determined to get there in as little time as possible, keeping her eyes on the blue light ahead, occasionally checking her phone.

The last mile of the trek took an hour and left her muscles aching as if she was on the home stretch of a marathon.

But at last, the tall rock face of the caverns appeared and she grit her teeth, pushing forward till she left the forest and stepped into the sunlight. At last, she was close enough to touch the smooth wall, leaning her forehead against it to rest for a moment.

*Pop!*

The blue light disappeared around her, rolling backward toward the forest. The pressure was relieved and she sucked in air through her teeth, leaning heavily against the wall. *Two p.m.* "How is that possible? Time is slipping away." She plucked Yumfuck off her shoulder and held him out in the palm of her hand to get a good look at him. His fur was covered in sweat and burrs clung to him. "You okay?"

"I've seen worse. Come on, let's get going. We're close now. Use the spell."

"The one spell Turner said I can use." Leira took another deep breath and stood back, looking up at the rock face to the caverns hundreds of feet in the air. "Altrea Extendia," she said with conviction. Bronze sparks erupted, creating a staircase that lead up to the middle opening. Leira started up the stairs, taking some of them two at a time, adrenaline kicking in, easing her aching body, as she got closer to the goal.

She stepped onto the wide ledge outside the opening and looked back as the stairs dissolved back into sparks, floating down to the ground below. "Here we go," she whispered and walked into the caves. *Follow your own instincts.* Turner's last instruction. She looked at each of the openings in front of her in the semi-darkness and felt a tug to the right, taking a step before she could think about it. On and on she went, the troll on her shoulder. Left, another left, then a right down a long, narrow passage too short for her to stand up all the way. Her eyes glowed and the symbols on her arms flipped over and over as she turned back and forth, back and forth in the narrow passageway till she finally arrived at an unexpected sight.

It was a wooden door in the middle of ancient caverns, curved at the top, painted red and set tightly into the wall. "The entrance to Oz," whispered Yumfuck from his perch on her shoulder.

Leira hesitated for only a moment and knocked hard three times, stepping back to wait. The handle turned and the door slowly swung open with a soft creak. Standing in the door frame was a slight figure thousands of years old and blind but could see far more than any other living creature.

"Come in, come in," said Tess, the ancient seer. Her long white hair was braided, hanging over her shoulder. Her chin was turned up toward Leira, but her eyes were a milky blue. "Time is of the essence and I have so much to tell you. I've been waiting for you for a very long time. A new journey is unfolding. Always exciting," she said in her high-pitched voice, already heading deeper into the chamber without a misstep despite her blindness.

Leira followed behind her, the door swinging shut with a soft click, the lock turning itself.

"I'm to be your next teacher," said Tess, settling herself into an overstuffed chair.

Leira stopped and took a look around at the room lit by soft candlelight. It looked like a living room from back in Austin. "How did you get all of this up here?"

"Turner Underwood is very clever. Come, find a seat and be quick about it." She held her thin, frail arms open wide. "We're still in the caverns and yet, we're not. Let's start with you telling me why you agreed to be here."

"There was a battle." Leira shook her head. "No, that's not quite right. There was a war that went on and on till it ended in a battle. Even the dead showed up to fight each other."

"Have a seat. This sounds like it's going to be a long story."

Yumfuck took the opportunity to jump down and make his way along the wall, searching for anything interesting. He disappeared around the corner letting out a loud cackle.

"Just a second," said Leira, about to follow the troll.

"Let him go. He'll be fine."

"Yes, but will this place? I don't suppose you've hidden any snacks around the place."

Tess let out a laugh and sat back. "Sit down. You don't have a lot of time till the sun goes down and I have a lot to teach you. Why are you here?"

Leira found a wooden ladderback chair and pulled it

closer, sitting down. "The battle wasn't going in our direction and if we lost, very bad things would come next. I couldn't let that happen." She fit her fingers neatly around her wrist where the bracelet used to be. "I let the light flow through me, without hesitation and almost died."

"Someone grounded you." Tess pressed her fingertips together in a steeple against her lips. "You were very lucky, but one detail in your story is incorrect. You wouldn't have died. You would have been absorbed and disappeared. There would have been no more *you*."

"Good to know." Leira pursed her lips, lightly drumming her fingers on the seat of the chair. "It was decided that there needs to be another way when things get fucked up. I have a mate now, Correk and there's Yumfuck," she said, leaning over to look down the hall. There was the sound of glass tinkling and small paws running but Tess didn't look concerned as Leira sat up straight. "Turner Underwood said you'd have a solution. A different kind of magic that might work just as well."

"Not might, does. Especially for someone with your unique combination of Jasper Elf and your own spark of humanity. So rare." Tess smiled deeply, the wrinkles deepening across her face. "If you are willing to learn, it is possible to harness the light and use it in moderation with another kind of magic even older than dark magic."

Leira slid to the edge of the seat.

"There is always magic all around us, even when your kind are not present. It lives in the ground, in the humble herbs and even in what most would call weeds." Tess clapped her hands together. "Oh, and the trees. The trees oversee it all and are their own artifacts, holding magic from other creatures and parceling it out so efficiently. Surely you've met a Dryad or two."

"Only one comes to mind. No one ever talks about humble magic. Earth is supposed to be absent of most magic till the gates open again. That is your prediction."

"Indeed. Technically true. That luxurious kind of magic that everyone can access without a thought, which feels so delicious." Tess gently shook her shoulders and smiled. "That will not be with us for thousands more years. But I never said there was no other kind. Natural magic was always here and will always be here but to access that one has to look for it and learn how to access it. Being able to channel energy is not enough. The arrogance of easy access has caused most to overlook the possibilities."

"Including me." Leira sat back in her chair. There was a yelp and a loud cheer from the other room. "Nothing to worry about," yelled the troll. "I've got it."

Leira slid forward again but Tess didn't move, and Leira settled back again. "How terrifyingly bad could it be?" she muttered.

"Including you," said Tess. "Nature is smart and knows how to protect itself. If natural magic was obvious there would be many who would try to use it for dark purposes with no concern for the source. The Gardener of the Dark Forest is a great practitioner of natural magic. You've seen it performed many times but attributed it to Oriceran magic."

Leira's eyes widened and she felt the magic stir in her feet.

"Ah, even awareness can start the connection between magic you know and magic you're about to discover. But..."

Tess held a finger in the air, turning it every which way. Leira felt the magic drift from one side of her body to the other with each turn. "The magic also listens to you. This is not a one-sided operation."

Tess laughed, pressing her hands against her knees. "Natural magic is a conversation anyone can have. There is still much you don't know about magical energy or even the world on which you live, which is good news. Better to live with the notion there is always more to learn." Tess arched an eyebrow and seemed to stare straight at Leira, making the magic inside rise up even further into Leira's chest. "The real question is, are you willing? Wait, wait," the old seer said, holding up a hand. "Don't answer too quickly. The road can be a hard one and willingness may wane. Natural magic will never bend to your will. It works in cooperation even in a crisis. That has frustrated many a practitioner in the past. You will not be the leader in this foray, but a follower or a partner at best, and always. It will take patience. Think about that and come back with an answer."

Leira looked around the cavern. "Back here?"

"If you decide your answer is yes, Turner Underwood will provide you with a back door of sorts. That will be the only short cut you get so treasure it. Till then, it's time to make your way back home. The sun will set before you know it and this can be a dangerous place at certain times. The darkness tonight is one of them."

Leira stood up, taking a step toward the rooms to find Yumfuck but Tess was already lighting some dried herbs in a clay bowl, blowing out the flames. The smoke rose in two strands curling around each other, quickly sliding to the right and down the hall.

A muffled, "Huh?" could be heard as the smoke started to blow in the opposite direction despite the lack of a breeze. At the tip of the smoke as it came back into the room was the troll, breathing in deeply. The smoke was curling around his ankles.

"Bring a notebook the next time. A pen will not be necessary. It will be part of our first lesson." Tess wet a finger and thumb and pinched the wick, the smoke disappearing just as suddenly as it appeared. The trance was broken and Yumfuck shook his head as Leira held out her hand. He climbed into her palm and she placed him in her pocket, nestled against a pale yellow wash cloth, soft with age. Leira bit her lip. "Thank you," she said as Tess nodded. She left without saying another word.

---

"Altrea Extendia," said Leira, standing on the edge of the outcrop and looking down at the uneven face to the ground far below. A bronze staircase appeared, weaving together as Leira started down, glancing at her watch. "Almost four o'clock. Two hours to go." She got to the ground and glanced back as the stairs disappeared, bronze sparks skittering across the ground.

She turned toward the forest in front of her. "Ready, Yumfuck?"

"Always," he chirped, poking his head out of the pocket. "Let's roll."

"Stay alert. The return trip may be even more interesting."

"Bring it, motherfuckers."

Leira strode across the open area and entered the woods, stepping across a tree root just as a branch leaned down to push her back. She ducked just in time, moving past the tree, sliding her foot before the root could wrap around her ankle. "Work together," she muttered. She stopped and stood still in the center of a copse of trees, already losing light from the heavy canopy over her head. The magic stirred in her feet, gently rising through her legs and up her body. Symbols flipped over and over again on her arms, glowing through the sleeves of her jacket. Her eyes glowed in the darkness illuminating the space in front of her. *Set an intention with the trees.* "Can I pass this way? I'm asking for your help. What is the best route?"

The wind picked up, tousling her hair. The trees creaked and swayed as Leira waited, the symbols along her arms flipping a little faster. A minute went by and she could feel Yumfuck getting restless, but she pressed a hand gently against her pocket to get him to stay still. She held out her hands in front of her, slowly opening her fingers as a ball of clear blue light formed. The trees swayed first toward the light and then gently away. Branches slightly to her left lifted creating an arch to pass through. Leira gently tossed the ball in the air and looked up in wonder as it paused a few feet above her head, lighting the new path in a gentle blue light.

"How did you know to do that?" whispered the troll, looking up at the light.

"I have no idea. Come on, a way has been made." She looked up at the trees. "Thank you."

"Onward!" shouted Yumfuck, standing up in her pocket. The branches rustled in response.

Leira stepped under the arch and made her way over the uneven ground already making better time. She was starting to breathe more easily, the minutes slipping away as she reached the riverbed and followed the path. But just as she got to the halfway point her boots began to sink again and the scar on her belly burned, making her wince. "There's more than one kind of magic in these woods. Something else is here." She pushed back her sleeve and looked at the symbols. "Dark magic rests here too. The light and the dark, they're always together somehow, balancing each other out. Not the best news for us at the moment."

The Jasper Elf and the troll trudged on, pushing through the pulsating energy working to slow them down. At last, they reached the bank of the river where they had entered. The trees were already folding back their branches even at the top, letting in more sunshine. Leira looked up and saw that the light was waning.

"It's five-thirty. There isn't much time left," she said, stepping up onto the bank. Yumfuck leaned out of her pocket, staring into the forest through the dim light. He hopped out and scrambled down her leg to the forest floor.

"Did you hear something?" asked Leira, still making her way. She stopped and turned around as the troll grew to match her size, a few feet shy of his largest size.

"Something isn't right." He twisted his head from right to left, sniffing the air. "There's a bitterness in the air.

Something acrid. Let's keep moving," he said in a low growl. "You go ahead of me. I'll keep watch from back here."

Leira hesitated, but only for a moment and started moving again, picking up as much speed as she could, pushing back against the waves of dark magic that were slowly increasing in the woods, weaving in and out. The bitter smell was crawling over everything the last mile through the woods.

They got to the edge of the woods at last and stopped at the clearing just in front of the parking lot. Leria felt the tentacles of magic trying to reach out and grab her. She held open her hand as small fireballs the size of marbles appeared. She threw them into the woods in an arc, watching them sizzle over the lines of dark magic, steam rising with contact. The energy pulled back just enough to let the pair run toward the rental car, sliding inside as Yumfuck shrunk back down to just three inches tall.

Leira quickly started the engine and glanced at her watch again. "Six o'clock." She leaned forward and looked out the windshield. The sun was setting just over the horizon. "Time to get the hell out of here." She turned the car around and sped up, looking up at the rearview mirror as the gravel flew out from beneath the wheels.

Behind them, the forest was disappearing into an inky darkness that bulged out in places. Blisters appearing on the veil that held the place between the living and the World in Between. Just as Leira got to the first turn she looked back again as a clawed hand reached out of the darkness. She quickly made the turn and pressed her foot down on the accelerator, not slowing down until she could feel the energy finally calming down.

"This is going to be a weird adventure, Yumfuck."

"My favorite kind." The troll stood on the button that let down his window with a steady hum. He rocked his head back, the wind blowing through his green fur, and let out a howl into the night. Nearby shifters answered the call letting out an eerie answer of their own as the car sped down the road.

## CHAPTER FOUR

"The directions said turn by the big oak." Leira looked over at Correk who was biting down on the end of a red licorice stick. "We're going to a crawdad boil and you're eating candy." She was driving down an old state highway shrouded by tall trees, following the signs for Redden State Forest deep in the woods of Maryland.

"It's tradition. We drove over an hour and left the city limits." He took another bite, filling his cheek. She looked down at the troll sitting between them. He was wearing his cowboy boots and had tied a licorice stick around his waist and was nibbling on one end. "Yeehaw, my friend," he said, giving her a wink.

Leira stopped the green Mustang at a fork in the road, leaning forward to gauge the size of the trees around them. "That has to be it. Right? She squinted up at the largest tree. That's a big oak, maybe. Where's my mother when you need her?" A rush of cool energy crept up into her lap and filled her chest. She felt herself relax. *Thanks Mom.* "Yep, that's a large ass oak."

She glanced over again and gave a crooked smile.

"You can spare one," argued Correk. He had one end of a nonpareil, the tiny white dots dropping onto the seat. Yumfuck had the other end in his teeth and was quickly winning the argument by eating his way to the other side. "Ow!" Correk drew back his thumb, looking for blood.

Leira turned the car, waving her hand over the pile of nonpareils in Yumfuck's lap, making them grow to three times their size.

"How long have you been able to do that?" Correk arched an eyebrow, pulling two of the larger nonpareils away from the troll who was hastily trying to lick them all. "Never mind. Don't care," said Correk, taking a large bite, wiping his mouth.

"For a while," she said, laughing. "I've been saving it for a special occasion. This is starting to look really special."

Yumfuck doubled down and spit on the remaining chocolate, drool cascading over the white sprinkles on the front.

"There's not enough cursed magic in the world that can get me to eat another one of those now." Correk let out a resigned sigh and dug through the bag between his feet for something else.

"You two are spending too much time together. Maybe." She turned her head away, suppressing a laugh. "Definitely," she muttered, as a faded blue pickup truck passed on the other side of the two-lane road. The back window was covered with plastic and silver electric tape. "Where did you hear about this place?"

"In my travels," said Correk, pulling a Starburst out of his pocket and quickly sliding it into his mouth even as

Yumfuck looked up, sniffing the air. "A grateful Wizard I rescued from some angry mermaids. He had tried to move the tide in his favor and things didn't go as planned."

Leira arched a brow and slowed down behind a truck pulling a short, open trailer packed with lawn mowers. "Kind of ambitious. He tried to influence an ocean. I get why they were angry."

"Don't mess with mermaids. They know magic that I don't think even Turner could figure out." Correk pulled another Starburst out of his pocket just as a small paw grasped the other end. He pulled the Starburst toward his mouth, even as Yumfuck dangled in the air, refusing to let go. "I'm willing to eat you whole," said Correk, looking Yumfuck in the eye.

"Ditto," said the troll, his mouth ringed in chocolate and candy dots still clinging to his fur. Yumfuck grasped the candy tighter, digging his claws in and pointed his toes, ducking his chin. "Try it," he squeaked.

"Okay, now I'm not hungry." Leira tilted her head and glanced over at Correk. "Seriously, hundreds of years of living in a royal court has come to this. Let it go."

"This isn't over," said Correk, as Yumfuck swayed in front of him. He plopped the troll back on the seat and let go of the orange Starburst.

The troll let out a satisfied whoop and held the Starburst over his head, congratulating himself.

"Don't push it," said Leira, "or I'll help him the next time."

"You should be helping me every time. We're a team." Correk thumped his chest with his fist.

"We're bonded." The troll smirked, turning around and

twerking in Correk's direction as he bit down on the chewy, sweet morsel.

Correk suppressed a smile and shook his head. "It's a wonder there is anything left to eat on Oriceran with all your cousins roaming freely."

"Tell me more about the gun range," said Leira, coming alongside a van with children pressing their faces against the glass. Yumfuck easily bound over Correk's lap, bouncing onto the door handle and landing at the bottom of the window. He pressed his sticky hands against the glass and opened his mouth wide, sticking out his tongue over his tiny, sharp teeth. A filmy swirl appeared on the glass.

"It's not really a gun range. More of a weapons range. A place for magicals to try out a new power."

The children squealed with delight at the troll's antics and pressed their mouths against the window, blowing out air to make their cheeks expand. Yumfuck fell back laughing, slipping off the door and landing neatly in Correk's lap. He quickly crawled back up to the door handle as Leira pulled ahead. She glanced over at Correk, her brows knitted.

"It happens sometimes. Elves grow into a power or somebody puts a hex on them that has a consequence no one sees coming. Then they need a safe place to figure out how to handle the new skill, or curse." He dried off a nonpareil on his pants leg and bit an edge. "What? I changed my mind."

Yumfuck glanced back and let out a cry. "Wooohooo!," he yelped with a wide grin, before licking a smear of chocolate off his fur.

"Okay, I'm really not so hungry anymore," muttered Leira.

"Why are you looking at me?" Correk brought his fingers together with a flash of golden light, erasing any trace of chocolate still sticking to his hand.

"Very clever. Do they even have napkins on Oriceran?"

"For show."

The troll stood on the button, lowering the window, crawling back up to the window's edge. The wind was blowing back his fur. "Ahoy motherfuckers," he yelled, waving at the van. The woman behind the wheel turned to look, her eyes growing wide just as Leira pressed her foot against the gas pedal.

"He's been on a sailing kick since he found out this was a crab boil." Correk gave a wave to the passing cars.

"That's not helping."

"Well, it's helping me."

Leira raised the window as Correk plucked the troll off the door. "He's an ambassador for swearing everywhere."

Correk smiled, "Then you're its prime minister."

"You sure Yumfuck should be on a magical gun range?" Leira looked in the rearview mirror at all the traffic slowing down to give them room. *Can't say I mind that.*

"Yumfuck knows how to handle himself around weapons of any kind. We've seen that before."

"I was thinking of the other magicals. He likes to get things going."

The troll looked up at Leira and let out a cackle. He was standing next to Correk's pocket, pulling on it but Correk had his hand pressed firmly against it.

"It's not easy to get a good fight going at the range.

Turner Underwood designed the place and there are hidden spells everywhere. More than one magical has found themselves back at home in an instant."

Yumfuck let out a sigh and shrugged, sitting down.

"I have a couple of spells I've wanted to try out." Leira felt a warm swirl of magic in her belly.

"Spells? That's not your usual gear."

"I'm adding to the skill set." She shook her wrist, the new bracelet jangling. "A plan B to make the nuclear option even less necessary."

Leira held her breath for a moment, not saying anything. *Hagan's old rule.* It was still a touchy subject between them. Correk set his jaw every time the topic of the last great battle came up. This was no exception.

His voice was low and calm, but Leira knew better. "Louie may have found you a new stone to stabilize the magic, but it's no guarantee." He hesitated, looking at her intently. "There is no plan where you are expendable." He turned and looked straight ahead at traffic but gently reached out to grasp her hand. "Ever," he whispered, the word catching in his throat.

Leira didn't bother trying to explain, again. He had held her tight every night since and she had whispered in the dark more than once that she wasn't trying to leave. Practicing spells was her way of letting him know, she was working on it. *I need to tell him about the seer.* Her lips pressed together in a thin line. *Maybe today.* The old scar on her belly warmed up for a moment, calming back down and her eyes flashed with light. She looked out her window, hiding the flash of magic as symbols crept down her arms. "What gets in the way of someone taking a cheap shot before they're transported home?" she asked, changing the subject.

"There are proctors at every station on the range just in case tempers even flicker. A variety of different magicals so no one can play favorites. The range is set up on a grid with clearly defined places to stand and they're marked with the kind of weapons you can use in each area. Veer from the guidelines and learn the consequences."

"A magical version of Children of the Corn."

"Not quite as punitive but close. Otherwise, a Kilomea would tear apart a Gnome and then all of his brothers would enchant their axes and boom! Mayhem."

"A regular Saturday night in some parts," laughed Leira, suddenly pointing. "There it is." A large billboard painted white with tall black letters appeared around a bend. *Remington Gun Range.* Leira looked at Correk, her brows knit together. "Humans are here?"

"Not exactly. Just wait, it will all make sense," said Correk, as Leira pulled the Mustang onto the gravel road. They passed by the oversized sign as a silvery shimmer passed over the car. Suddenly, a field appeared where there had been trees. It was lined with cars and there were magicals milling about everywhere. Some had enhanced weapons slung over their shoulders, heading for the ranges that were now visible in the distance. A sign, *Warlock'd and Loaded* was suspended high in the air over the road, glittering silver in the sunlight.

"That's better," laughed Leira, steering the Mustang onto the grass, jostling over the uneven terrain.

Yumfuck bounced on the center console between the seats, striking a pose with one fist outstretched. "Faster than a speeding bullet!" he chirped, landing on one knee only to pop up again, floating just into view to other drivers, striking a different pose. "I am Batfuck," he growled, landing again. "Ooh, where's my utility belt?"

"It's in your backpack, along with your cape and mask." Leira found a spot near the front just as someone else was leaving. "Still works, even in a crowd of magicals," she muttered, a crooked smile passing across her face. She stopped the car and got out, stretching her arms overhead.

Correk got out with the troll balanced on his shoulder. The troll was wearing his small navy-blue backpack bulging at the seams. Correk slid out a tall bow from the back seat and balanced it on his shoulder.

An eight-foot troll lumbered past, the blue pile of hair spiked with gel for extra effect. Trailing him were a dozen other six-inch trolls taking shortcuts under cars and around moving feet, hitching rides on unsuspecting magicals, leaping from one car hood to another. "Lsai, keep up!" The smallest of the trolls with a shock of orange hair ran as fast as she could, tumbling over and over, rolling toward the group. The bigger troll let out a low protest that rumbled the ground as he leaned back and scooped Lsai up in mid-step, trudging past a large wooden sign that had been burned down on the right side leaving, *Fireball Range*, and the image of a Wood Elf with an upraised arm, but no hand.

"That was something to see. Can trolls bond to each other?" Leira watched the odd parade as the large troll made his way to the far right sector still a long way off.

"Too many opportunities to rescue a troll or two and take home a family of them." No one answered her.

Correk was already waving to another Light Elf who had a long bow strapped to his back. The troll was jumping up and down on Correk's shoulder, clapping his tiny paws.

"Okay, read the room. I get it. Fun day. I can do fun. What?" She caught Correk smiling at her as she flexed her hands.

"Nothing. I appreciate your enthusiasm."

Leira arched a brow and sent a fine spray of tiny fireballs around his feet.

"Hey! That's a violation of the rules," laughed Correk, hopping back and forth. "Great way to get yourself kicked out. That's not your plan, is it?" He smiled, wrapping Leira into a tight hug as she broke into a grin. Yumfuck kissed the top of her head.

"See ya'!" squealed the troll, sliding down Correk's arm and making the leap to the ground, running after the other trolls. "Hey Manny, is that you?" He easily caught up to the cluster of furry creatures as the large troll turned around and gave him a salute. Lsai was still riding in his oversized palm.

Correk adjusted his bow and started weaving between the cars, his arms pumping. "No, that's the one magical they can't bond to. And yes, someone goes home from here with a troll all the time. It's almost like a parting gift."

"Very wrong," muttered Leira, careful to watch where she stepped in case there was a small, stray troll lagging behind. "I love you, *and* Yumfuck, but one's enough."

"What do you feel like doing first? Fireballs or fighting

off spells?" Correk rebalanced the bow hanging from one shoulder.

Leira smiled at him, letting out the breath she had been holding in. "Go, hang with the other elves at the archery range. I'm assuming there's one of those here? I'll be fine. I'll get the lay of the land. What's the worst that can happen?" She patted Correk's startled expression. "Kidding. It's me. I don't cause trouble. I just clean it up. Go," she said, gently pushing him toward the range.

Leira watched him go, waving when he turned back to look just once. She pushed her bangs off her forehead. "Food first, then look for trouble."

Off to the side, far from the different weapons areas were large boiling pots sitting over wood fires. A Gnome was already pouring out the contents of one pot, grunting as he spilled large bright red crabs onto a long table covered in brown paper. Magicals of all kinds stepped up to grab a few of the crabs before they were all gone.

"Okay, I can do fun," muttered Leira, pushing her way through the thin crowd and piling crabs onto a thick paper plate. Her eyes took on a warm glow and symbols appeared on her arm. "What now?" She glanced down, expecting the worst. Time to go and far too early. "We need this break."

But a crooked smile grew on her face instead. "This is a first. My early warning system is actually predicting a good day. Why does that make me even more nervous?" Memories of the last battle slipped through her mind, sending a shudder down her back and shaking the plate. A crab began to fall and a passing dwarf caught it, biting it in half and smiling at Leira. "Thanks!"

Leira took in a deep breath and held it for a moment before letting it go. "I really may have forgotten what fun looks like. Fuck."

A general roar and gasps went up from a crowd across the parking lot, closer to the archery range. Leira put down the plate, ignoring the wizards and gnomes fighting over it. She walked as fast as she could without breaking into a run toward the commotion. But soon enough, her legs gave in and began running easily, taking her across the uneven ground till she got to the edge of the crowd that was pushing toward the Light and Wood Elves who were all standing aside, watching one magical in particular.

"Correk." Leira pushed her way through, letting the magic go first to make a way.

Correk was standing at the firing line holding up an arrow. "Three times was plenty. Look, we're drawing a crowd. I'm not doing it again."

Yumfuck was dancing along the shaft of the arrow, making faces at Correk, his tiny paws on his hips. "One more and you can have your Hershey bar back."

"I knew you took it."

Leira felt tears fill her eyes and brushed them away. "No one you love is in trouble." She patted her chest. *Tap, tap, tap.*

"Fine," said Correk, nocking the arrow in place, the troll sliding down till he was lying flat against the shaft away from the bow string. "But I want the whole box."

"Whatever's left of it. Let 'er rip!" the troll squealed as Correk slowly drew back.

The arrow let go with a sound *thwack*, whistling through the air with Yumfuck holding as tight as he could, his arms and legs wrapped tightly. Leira could hear a faint, "motherfucker" as the arrow sped toward the target.

The arrow found the bullseye with the troll still attached landing neatly in the middle of the bullseye. There was general applause for Correk's aim but everyone was really waiting to see how the troll fared. Yumfuck shook his head and shoulders, wiggling his arms and stood up on the arrow, raising his paws in triumph, shaking them over his head. The crowd cheered, holding up a wide assortment of weapons. Many of them glowing from magical enhancements.

The troll dropped neatly to the ground and ran through the thick grass back to Correk, scrambling up his pant leg until Correk scooped him up and put him on his shoulder. "Pay up," he said, finally noticing Leira in the crowd, an easy smile coming across his face.

Leira smiled back and glanced down at the still-moving symbols on her arm. All good news.

The troll held onto Correk's collar and swung around till he was inches from his nose, staring into his eyes. "I have half of one left and it's all yours." Yumfuck shrugged. "To show I'm a straight shooter--" The troll clapped his hands on his shaking belly as he laughed at his own joke. "I won't eat any more of the ones you're saving in the trunk."

"In the trunk? You found the ones in the trunk?"

Yumfuck said nothing and instead licked his lips, scrambling down Correk's side, and jumping to the ground. The troll ran into the dense crowd without looking back.

"You have to get back in the car sometime," yelled Correk, holding up his bow.

Leira smiled, walking over to Correk and relaxing into his chest, letting him wrap his muscled arms around her. The Light Elf kissed the top of her head. "Miss me already?"

"Always," said Leira, the feeling of approaching trouble still lingering across the back of her neck.

## CHAPTER FIVE

Harkin ambled across the large grounds of the protected sanctuary, working his way into the hundred-acre dense forest cared for by the Gardener of the Dark Forest just east of Austin, Texas. Tiny pixies accompanied him, flitting around his shoulders or riding on top of his head. Their slender wings were glowing in the early morning light.

The Light Elf stopped at the edge of a lake and took off his tunic, carefully folding it and leaving it at the water's edge. Thick, ropey scars crossed his broad back, some faded from time and others pink and shiny that spoke of more recent troubles. Harkin stepped into the cool waters, sucking in air between his teeth as his skin adjusted to the temperature. He walked in further and further till only his head was above water, his long grey hair trailing behind him.

He ducked down, submerging and began to swim long, easy, powerful strokes toward the bottom. A few of the pixies were still sitting on his head, taking the ride with him. He came to an abandoned mine shaft and kept swimming, entering into the inky darkness.

The path was so familiar by now he was able to keep going without slowing down, hugging first the wall to the left and then the wall to the right to avoid old debris as the mine slowly collapsed. Only magic was holding up the rotten beams now.

He came to a turn in the tunnel and stopped, pressing on the nearby moss-covered wall. It easily gave way, opening into an anteroom full of light that shone brightly into the mine, illuminating the small fish darting everywhere.

Harkin pulled himself in the rest of the way, letting the door close with a loud click behind him.

The lake water quickly drained away as Harkin shook out his wet hair and smoothed it back, waiting till the room was empty. He opened the next door, passing into a space with a towel and a fresh tunic and got himself dressed.

Beyond that door was his new lab, well hidden from the world and known only to two magicals. The Gardener and his son, Correk. The new Fixer. Harkin couldn't have hidden it from him, even if he had wanted to and he definitely wanted to but hid it as well as he could. He needed to, to keep his new project a secret for as long as he could, especially from Correk.

He went to a metal door with a window and unlocked it, stopping at the threshold to look around the room, yet again. "I am not very good at learning from the past." He rubbed his beard with a meaty palm.

Situated squarely in the center of the narrow room was

a clear, pressurized box long enough to contain the body of a female Light Elf in suspended animation. Glowing gold and purple-striped caterpillars inched along her arms and legs regularly emitting electrical signals that were picked up by a nearby tall, narrow computer.

Harkin placed his hand on the side of the box, splaying his fingers. The same worried look he carried on his lined face most days. "Robin, my first love. My only love. Always a sign of everlasting spring. Who did this to you? How do I get you back? Your son misses you, too, but he's sure you're dead. Gone for so long now." He rested his forehead just over her face, staring down at her for the hundredth time. "I found you again. After all these years. I can't let you go, and I will find a way to bring you back, or go mad trying." He gave an uneasy laugh. "Come back to me," he said, straightening up and turning around to read the new data. "Nothing. What dark magic is this?"

CHAPTER SIX

Louie waited for Ava to take her seat before handing her the tall plastic cup of Bare Bones beer with the Washington Nationals logo on the front. The Nats were playing the Marlins and Louie had managed to trade an old artifact that had long run out of any magic for two seats tucked up high and to the left.

"This is great, right?" He squinted at the playing field below, trying to follow the arc of the ball before it landed in an outfielder's mitt.

Ava took a long sip and smiled, foam clinging to her top lip. "The best," she said, taking another long sip. "Sit." She patted the hard plastic seat next to her. "You did good. Enjoy the game, with me. Down here," she said as the crowd cheered.

Louie slid into his seat, leaning forward, the beer sloshing around in the cup.

"Hey! Hey!" A red-faced portly man in a tight, grey t-shirt that dug into his muscular arms twisted in place, leaning his hand on the empty seat next to him. "What the hell?" He held up his hands as if beer was dripping off them, instead of just the sprinkling across the back of his shoulders.

"Sorry dude, my fault. I got caught up in the action." Louie tried smiling. His charm had gotten him out of worse scrapes with hairier beasts. Kilomeas, angry Gnomes with axes. At least made them hesitate.

Not this time.

"That's it? That's all you got?" He ran a wide hand with stubby fingers through clipped brown hair and started to rise.

Louie carefully set down his beer, tucked just under the frame of his seat and slowly stood. He started to take a step in front of Ava when she surprised him, reaching out her small hand and lightly pressing it against the man's shoulder. "All is well," she whispered. "You love being at a baseball game. Nothing can lower your enthusiasm. Everyone is your friend."

The large man let out a small squeak, his hazel pupils dilating in a full bloom before settling back again. His furry eyebrows working themselves up and down his forehead.

Louie felt the swirl of magic rubbing against his ankles, connecting him to Ava and then the stranger. A familiar rush of adrenaline shimmied up his spine, curling around the energy. He felt himself relax, settling into familiar territory. A small strategic skirmish with no rules.

"A bonum conquiescamus--"

"No!" Ava spit out the word, spreading her fingers wide in the air before making a circular motion, one hand following the other. Louie felt the push of energy and for a moment saw the deep purple of Ava's magic flow up against his. A deep, shimmering bronze. She gave a hard shake of her head, her chin lifted.

"That's not good," muttered Louie. He had seen that look before.

The large Nats fan in front of them shook his head, his cheeks shaking. He was still twisted in his seat, looking up at Louie but with a quizzical look, like he forgot what he was doing. He suddenly smiled, revealing a row of perfect tiny teeth that didn't match the large head. "Great game, huh?" he offered, turning around without waiting for an answer. He took a deep breath and let it out with a shudder, settling into his seat.

"What did you think you were doing?" whispered Ava. "I didn't ask for your help."

"Neither did I." Louie bit his lower lip, resisting the urge to smile. He wanted to take back the words, but it was too late.

Ava narrowed her gaze, staring into his eyes for a moment too long. "True, but I wasn't thinking of you."

A wiry teenager in cargo shorts that dwarfed his thin legs, and a Jimmy Buffet t-shirt worked his way to the empty seat in front of them and sat down, handing a small baseball hat filled with strawberry ice cream to the formerly angry fan. "Here, Dad. Nothing but strawberry. Just the way you like it. Hope you like it." There was a nervous tremor to his voice.

The man raised a large arm and swung it around his son, pulling him closer, surprising the young man. "It's always a good day when it's watching baseball with you." He let out a contented sigh, resting the plastic hat on his leg. "Go Nats!" he bellowed.

Louie felt every muscle tense as he watched the kid's face bloom into a smile staring at his father. The boy turned to the game and shot a fist into the air. "Go Nats!" he yelled, his voice breaking halfway, looking back to his father.

The man smiled and drew his son closer. "A very good day."

"I have a lot to learn," muttered Louie.

Ava leaned closer, wrapping her arm around Louie's. "Yes, you do. You are not the guide, not yet. If you want to master the spark, you will need to be able to take in all the possibilities around you. Not just your own agenda. Make it about you and you cut off the possibility of unexpected change."

Louie sat back and leaned down to pick up his beer. "That may take some doing."

"Then you're in luck." Ava leaned across the metal arm rest and kissed Louie's cheek. "We have plenty of time."

But there it was again. A rustling of energy across Louie's back. Nothing really, but it felt like a warning and Louie didn't ignore warnings. That's why he was still alive, after all. It didn't matter that the alarm was so quiet. Those were just the first inklings, something is wrong. *Pay attention.* He took a slow sip of his beer and looked around at the nearby crowd. Nothing out of the ordinary.

*I need to find Leira.*

The thought had tugged at him for days, but he had ignored it. "Just a little longer," he said quietly, swinging an arm around the back of Ava's chair, lightly resting his fingers on her small, round shoulder.

"What?" Ava looked up, distracted by the umpire calling a strike.

"It's a great day," he said, flashing a smile and kissing her before going back to watching the game. *Find Leira. Tomorrow.*

## CHAPTER SEVEN

Ariana stood on the verdant hill, turning her face into the wind rolling across the Kentucky estate. The sun was just beginning to set, turning the sky into streaks of purple and orange against the blue. Strands of her long, dark hair lifted in the breeze before resting against her bare shoulder.

"You'll catch something out here dressed like that." Uncle Felix walked up the sloping hill to stand next to Ariana.

"Witches don't catch anything." The head of the Dark Families pulled the skirt of her long dress around and out of the way of Uncle Felix's feet. "We hunt things down."

Uncle Felix gave a low chuckle and looked out over the large estate. Horses were running in a nearby field, keeping close to the fence line. "Not so much, lately. Peace treaties will do that to a good time."

Ariana folded her arms across her chest and let out a deep sigh. She was used to his baiting. "We lost too many of our own kind already, Uncle Felix. Give it a minute. We need to rebuild our ranks, tend to our wounded."

"Dig out some new spells." Uncle Felix squinted into the last of the light, rubbing his chin.

"I will do whatever is necessary." Ariana untucked a hand and let the pale, slender fingers roll out one at a time, a small blue flame appearing and dancing on the end of each finger. She raised her hand over her head, curled to the left, bringing it down to the right, creating an arc of flames over the pair's heads. The breeze passing through the flames instantly became warm against her skin.

"Treaties can be very useful. They don't have to last forever." Ariana rubbed her shoulder. "For now, Leira and I have made peace. It's the right thing to do."

Uncle Felix opened his mouth to protest but Ariana held up a manicured finger. "We have better things to do right now than an endless war with Leira Berens. Admit when something isn't working Uncle Felix. That attitude is what got my predecessor killed and burned down our library. In the end, we got nothing for our efforts but weakened ranks."

"*One* of our libraries, and not even one of the really good ones." There was no mention of the losses. Uncle Felix snapped his fingers and blew into his hand, holding his arm out straight. Fireflies appeared in his palm, taking flight, only to be followed by another handful, repeating the process till the field in front of them was filled with tiny, blinking yellow lights. He moved his hands through the air, orchestrating their movement, delighting himself. "Nature really is a wonderful thing. So complex and brilliant. So easily manipulated in the right hands."

A cold smile came across Ariana's face, still watching the sunset. "Nature will only let you do that for so long before it will slap you in the head. I've warned you before, Uncle," she said with a weary sigh. "Drama always was your forte. But sometimes pragmatic is what's called for to win the advantage. You want to take over the Dark Families, learn to play the long game."

Uncle Felix coughed, the smile freezing in place as the fireflies continued to dance in pockets of three or four, creating a large swirling, bobbing cloud of warm light.

"Don't bother saying anything." Ariana brushed her hair back, the dark cascade dangling just below her waist. "And quit trying, for now. I'm not going anywhere, anytime soon." She looked at her Uncle who was fixated on the flashing lightning bugs. "I'm sure your treachery will pay off eventually." Ariana whispered a short, dark spell unknown to anyone but the leader of the dark families.

The Kentucky grass at Uncle Felix's feet crept up his legs, quickly wrapping him tight, reaching around his neck till all that was showing were his eyes, wide with fear, and his nose trying to pull in enough air.

Just as quickly the grass receded back down beneath his feet. He took one long, shuddering breath trying to sputter out a response, but nothing was forthcoming.

"Stand up straight, Uncle and reclaim your false pride." Ariana took a long look at him, up and down. A cold stare that was merely a measurement. "Remember this moment and take note that was a throwaway spell. A nothing. There are thousands more I have already memorized, practiced and can draw on at a moment's notice."

The older wizard finally managed to suck in larger

gulps of air, a sheen of sweat across his forehead. The fireflies were forgotten, drifting away on the breeze to another pasture. Uncle Felix worked his neck and straightened the lapels of his ever-present dark jacket. "I have a proposal." He shook his head, pressing his eyelids shut before opening them to look at the last of the setting sun. "A practical one." Ariana turned her attention back to him and he winced, regretting the tell.

"Go on," she said, slowly. The darkness of the moonless night was gathering around them. Stars were appearing overhead, dotting the entire sky.

"You may not want a war with Leira Berens, but I know you still have the same plan that every leader before you has had for generations. Reinstall the Dark Families as the true leaders of magic."

"That is not much of a secret. Even that abominable troll that goes everywhere with the Jasper Elf knows that about us." Ariana snapped her fingers, lifting her hand. A warm light appeared just ahead of her lighting the walk back to the main house.

"We need to create an elite group of witches and wizards who can be trained to turn perception of events in our favor. Especially since there's a truce. Use the image of the kinder, gentler Dark Families to our advantage. They can become our ambassadors whispering just the right thing. Why use magic and show our hand in such an obvious way when we can use words more effectively."

Ariana had stopped walking and even taken a few steps back to the wizard. Her expression had changed, even if only a smidgen in his favor. "A different kind of Fixer." The corners of her mouth curled up. "It would need to be subtle. Make the fabric that holds everything together out there fray at the edges, unravel slowly." Ariana turned to go, stepping carefully along the path, over the damp grass. "The long game, Uncle Felix," she said over her shoulder. She turned her head toward the large house and the outlying barns. "One day, dear Uncle, we will have it out, at last and you will finally respect my powers or this time the grass will continue to grow." She marched forward, her head up, bracing herself for what was next.

Most of it, she would be the cause, but even Uncle Felix would not see it coming.

## CHAPTER EIGHT

"You need to see this. Now, right now." Correk was tugging at Leira's sleeve, reaching for her hand and pulling her toward a hastily made portal.

"What? See what? Do we need Yumfuck?" Leira pulled away, looking over her shoulder at the stairs. The troll was upstairs in his room, riding the tiny roller coaster that ran along the top of his walls. Leira could hear the small metal wheels grinding against the track.

"No, we don't need Yumfuck, not yet. We won't be there long." Correk wrapped his arm around Leira's waist and pulled her close, making his way quickly through their small kitchen toward the open portal.

Leira felt the energy scooping out of the ground and rising into her body, her eyes suddenly glowing. The magic swirled around in her belly, warming the old scar. "It's that dangerous," she muttered, "you need my help."

Correk looked back at her, and she saw something she rarely ever saw in his eyes. Fear mixed with anger. The only other time was at that battle, and then it was almost too late. But things were different. She had made a promise and Wolfstan was dead. The Dark Families were laying low, for now.

He pulled her through the portal, the sides quivering and faces from the World in Between pressing against the thin veil that separated them from this world. The Fixer Elf knew what he was doing and got Leira quickly through the space, ignoring the pleas. There was nothing even a Fixer could do for those trapped in that mire.

Leira couldn't stop herself from searching the faces as they sped past them. *Ossonia? Where are you? I'm sorry.* But there were no familiar faces. She stepped through to the narrow, dark alley surrounded by brick buildings that only stretched three floors into the air. "Where are we? There's no one here." Leira could feel her heart race quicken and knew, somehow, that was a lie. The energy knew something was amiss.

The symbols on her arms appeared, rolling slowly as if they were trying to figure out a puzzle with a few missing, key pieces. "That never happens," she whispered, feeling her chest tighten. "Correk, something's not right."

"I know." He stopped short, midway down the alley where there was a split, a connecting alley running in the other direction. "Come on," he said, taking a sharp left, his hand still grasping Leira's. "Do you smell that?"

Leira raised her chin, taking in short bits of air. "Yes, is that the ocean? It can't be. Where are we?" She was jogging to keep up with Correk's long, determined strides. A feeling of paranoia hung in the alleyway. There was something about it she recognized. A particular brand of creeping fear.

"Chicago in Lincoln Square. I was called here to help a Gnome who owed the wrong people, but this happened." They were only a few yards down the second alley. Correk put out his arm to stop Leira from taking another step, but she had already smelled the familiar odor wafting through the air. The tangy, damp smell jerked her head back and instinctively she held up a hand, a fireball appearing, then quickly extinguishing itself. There was no point. Weapons had never worked on the Dark Mist.

Just down the cross alley, bubbling in the center of the paved area the familiar dark, inky goop was writhing and twisting, rising up in peaks as if it was greeting someone familiar. Leira felt the same tug in the center of her body, trying to drag her toward the Dark Mist. "Is this the smell? Why would you bring me here?" she hissed. "Fuck this. This never goes well. What is there to learn from battling this thing one more time?"

"No, there's something else. That, that is something new." Correk nodded at the nearby brick wall and the graffiti spread across it. The Dark Mist was oozing over the wall, receding from it while leaving sharp images in its place. Glowing slash marks that didn't seem to add up to anything.

"I can't read any of it."

"It's an ancient Oriceran language. A Jasper Elf language long forgotten that very few remember. Turner Underwood taught me the basics. He said it was going to come in handy one day." Correk swallowed hard. "It says, *I'm coming for you.*' Over and over again."

"Fuck me. That's not possible. The Dark Mist isn't sentient. It still isn't, right? That thing isn't actually throwing down challenges." Leira looked at the symbols on her arms. They were starting to pick up speed, working out different outcomes that kept changing. None of them good.

"Leira, look closer. There's something else among the writing. There." Correk pointed toward the bottom left corner of glowing slash marks. There in the center of the pattern was something different.

"A severed hand. No. No, no, no. It can't be. That's impossible. Wolfstan is dead."

"No, Wolfstan disappeared. The only thing we ever found of him was his hand."

"None of this means it's him, back from the oozing dead-ish."

"Leira, you can feel it. Something is very off. It has been for days."

"Weeks. I've felt it for weeks."

"And you said nothing? We're partners."

Leira put her hand on his face, running her fingertips against the beginnings of his rough beard. The memories of that battle were still there, haunting them both. "There was nothing to say. It was just a feeling. This is a dangerous world and there's always some kind of danger, especially for us."

"Not like this."

"Still doesn't mean it's Wolfstan. He's not that powerful. No way he commandeered the fucking mother ship. It's a weird coincidence. Besides, how would he know the Jasper language? Everything, including magic, has to eventually make sense. The balance."

Leira saw Correk clench his fist and then let it go. *He's still angry. I did this.*

"Then something worse than the Dark Mist has taken it over and it's hunting you." Anguish filled his voice.

"Correk, we'll figure it out--"

"Leira, I'm the Fixer." Correk tapped his chest hard, his face pressed close to hers. "I can be anywhere, do almost anything, help anyone." He was biting off the words, bitter in his mouth. "But I have no idea what to do here. For you."

Leira looked at the pain in his face and reached out, wrapping her arms around him, squeezing tight. "Together," she whispered in his ear. "We fight on together. I promise. I will never do that again. Ever. I will not leave you out." She pulled her head back till she could see his face. She put a hand on his chest and let his energy blend with hers, sharing his pain. Her eyes filled even as she tilted up her chin. "I made a mistake and I hurt you. It was the very thing I was trying to prevent."

"I can't control any of this." Correk leaned down and she rested her forehead against his. "I don't even know if magic will work against whatever this thing is becoming," he said.

"Then we figure it out. We will fight this together. And somewhere in this mess, we find Ossonia and bring her home."

"If it is Wolfstan, we need my father. Harkin may know something."

"I have a few new tricks. Turner Underwood made an introduction to the old seer to make sure I have choices."

She felt him tense. One more thing she had waited to tell him. *Let it go, please.* "I'm learning from Tess. We aren't defenseless. If it's the last good thing we do," she whispered. *Please don't let it be Wolfstan.* Leira glanced down at her arm, watching the spiraling symbols, still searching for answers.

## CHAPTER NINE

Leira sat in the kitchen of their row house in D.C., her feet up on the table, sipping coffee. The day was just starting but Yumfuck had been up for hours, hammering away at something. Overhead she heard a delighted squeal and the rumbling of the racetracks followed by a distinct *tap, tap, tap.*

"What else could he fit in that room?" She shook her head. "Nope, don't ask that," she said, taking another sip of coffee. She looked up again at the ceiling and the sound of falling plaster. Pinpricks of dust motes floated down in front of her. "Nope. Nope."

"Why is your hand covering your mug?" Correk walked into the kitchen, yawned and stretched his arms over his head, looking up at the sound of more hammering. "Got it. He's remodeling again. Turner Underwood will love what we've done to his place."

"He could change it into a boathouse on a river with two stomps of that cane." Leira reached out her hand, intertwining her fingers with Correk's. "How's things?"

Their way of checking in with each other lately that didn't press too hard on any soft places.

"Things are okay." Correk crouched in front of Leira, still holding her hand. "You are my mate. I trust you with my life. If you say, you'll never try that again, I believe that's your intention."

Leira swung her feet down from the table. "That's a big plot twist you put at the end of that last sentence."

"You want it to be true, I know you do." He let out a deep sigh. "If someone you love is in trouble and there's nothing else you can do, can you promise me, on my life," he said, gently tapping his chest with her grasped hand, "that you wouldn't risk everything you have to try and save them? Even if you are obliterated from this world and the next?"

Leira felt the magic trying to clamber up her legs. "I gave you my word." *Keep your breathing steady, work with the energy.*

"Even if it was Estelle, or Mara or even Eireka? You'd stop just short of doing everything?" He held her hand tighter. "What if it were me?"

Leira glanced over the top of his head. "Don't ask that of me." She looked back at his face, a tear rolling down her cheek. "I still remember what you did for me on Enchanted Rock. Do you remember how you almost died?" Her voice was low and quiet, but she knew Correk could see right through her. The wound that never healed. "They took you away to Oriceran so fast I didn't even get to say goodbye. I had to wait for weeks to get word if you were going to be okay. To know if you would come back to me?"

The magic was still stirring, making its way into her

body, insisting on being acknowledged. Ever since the last, great battle the magic had become more insistent, looking for the danger. *Magic works both ways. Feel the balance.* "Do you regret saving my life?" she asked, gently. She tilted her head to one side, this time refusing to look away.

Correk gave a tired laugh and let go of her hand, reaching out to wrap his arms around her and pull her close, tightening his grip. "Never," he whispered in her ear, his nose pressed into her hair. He sat back on his heels and held her chin in his hand. "There's no real solution to our dilemma, is there?"

Leira slowly shook her head. "No, there isn't. We're not the kind of people who can sit on the sidelines, and the monsters we take on have enough bite to reshape the world." She leaned over and softly kissed Correk's forehead. "You're right," she said. "I can't absolutely promise I won't do whatever it takes to save someone I love, especially you. I suppose all I can do is get better at asking for help and taking it." She shrugged, trying to smile. "Maybe that will make a difference."

"I'm glad you are learning from Tess."

Leira's forehead wrinkled and she studied Correk's face. He was gently smiling. "Thank you," she whispered.

A green blur swung down from the ceiling, landing on Correk's head with a battle cry. "I am Batfuck!"

Correk fell back and landed with a thud on the kitchen floor, swearing in Oriceran and swatting at Yumfuck. The troll screeched in delight, running back and forth across Correk's head, just out of reach, whooping loudly with each near miss.

Leira pulled in her legs, laughing and resting her chin

on her knees. "You're only giving him what he wants, Correk," she said, grinning.

"He smells like sawdust and chocolate. What have you been doing up there?"

"Nothing!" Yumfuck leapt off Correk's head, spreading his arms wide, a blue cape billowing out behind him, and soaring just far enough to land on the top of Leira's knee. He slid down, deeper into her lap, hidden from Correk, still chortling and letting out his own version of war cries.

Correk pushed his hair off his damp forehead, his chest rising and falling as he caught his breath.

"You don't work this hard saving wizards from their own dark spells." Leira smiled at Correk and scooped up the troll, safely depositing him in her shirt pocket.

Correk started to say something but hesitated, turning his head to the left and listening to something only he could hear. Even Yumfuck grew still, waiting.

"I know that look," said Leira. "Go Fixer. Do your thing."

"A magical is killing poachers. Whoever it is, they're good. Not leaving a trace."

Leira slid her feet down to the floor. "I thought you could always sense where a magical had been, was going and where they were now. Like basic Fixer magic."

"It's not one hundred percent. Not for me yet, anyway. I have to go."

Leira gave him a nod, but he was already halfway through a portal. Damp, humid air leaked into the kitchen, hovering near the ceiling and large, leafy ferns bent into the room and back again. He was gone before she could say anything else.

"The Dark Gardener," she said, looking down at

Yumfuck who was leaning out of her pocket. "He would have that kind of magic to evade detection." She slowly shook her head. "No, he wouldn't do something like that?" *Perrom. Please don't let it be him. Ossonia, we need you back.*

Her phone buzzed on the table. She picked it up and caught a glimpse of her arm. The symbols lit up and then retreated. "Hello General Anderson. Something gone wrong in the world again?"

"Leira," he said, an obvious strain in his voice. "A day I thought I'd never see." He sighed. "What a ridiculous thing for me to say. How many days have there already been like that?"

Leira waited quietly for the old General to get to the point. He had earned at least that much.

"I'm afraid it's the Silver Griffins," he said at last.

"More dead?" The magic jumped forward, the symbols returning to her arms and the glow returning to her eyes.

"Unfortunately, yes, but not why I'm calling you. Some of the Silver Griffins have decided to take a darker path. They've formed a new group to seek out the bad element killing their comrades." Another deep sigh.

*Are you okay?* Leira wanted to ask her old friend, but he would never admit to anything. Best to keep going.

"They've managed to slip the knot of the Silver Griffins. Frankly, I thought that was impossible. I don't know. This magical stuff always seems to have endless loopholes."

Leira absently pressed a hand against her belly. "You have a mission for me?"

The General cleared his throat. "Yes, right! Find them before this goes too far. There have already been skirmishes and a few dead dark magicals. I can't say that's ruined my day, but this could all get out of hand very quickly. Find them!"

"And do what with them?"

There was a long pause. "If they can be reasoned with--" Another bit of silence. "Let them go. They've suffered enough. If not, do what you have to do." The General hung up before Leira could ask anything else. She set the phone down just as the troll peeked out of her pocket and looked up at her. "Go, I'll be fine. I have things to do," he squeaked.

Leira stared down at him. "I may need you on this one."

The troll climbed onto her shoulder, still wearing his cape. "Just send out the signal. I'll be there. Forever and always."

## CHAPTER TEN

The witch rubbed her thumb over the faded tattoo on the inside of her wrist. Two silver letters entwined into a curving S and G.

"Are you ready, Lizzie?" asked the burly Gnome, thick, curly brown hair growing down his bare arms that too closely resembled fur. Even the stained, red tank top looked like it was barely containing a miniature hair forest.

He held up the magnetic coil tattoo machine with the needle firmly in place and the tiny cups of red ink. "I have a line and you have places to be." He arched a brow and tilted his bald head. Lizzie squeezed her eyes shut and nodded her head. Her long, thick, gray hair fell forward across her face. "Do it, Finley." She pressed the two large gold coins in her other hand, the edges digging into her skin.

Finley grunted and adjusted the light over the witch's wrist, displaying a surprising light touch as he lowered the machine and the needle began tap, tapping away against Lizzie's skin.

Lizzie sucked in her stomach from the sharp pin pricks

but held still.

Slowly the red overtook the silver leaving it as only an accent against the new, emerging letters. The S became an R with sharper edges and the G became an upside-down elegant P, still entwined and easily hidden when necessary.

Minutes ticked by as Finley stopped to examine his artwork, turning her wrist and then beginning again, adjusting the edges and adding the tiniest filigree. "Uh huh, yup," he would say from time to time, gently but firmly holding the machine as it lightly bounced against Lizzie's skin.

Finally, he sat back, gently setting down his machine and slapping his wide, muscular thighs with both hands. "Done," he said, with a satisfied smile that showed more than one gold tooth surrounding his molars along the right side. A common affectation among Gnomes from the mountains of Oriceran. "You are now officially a Red Phoenix. The Silver Griffins are no more."

Lizzie held out her wrist, annoyed. The artful R and P were surrounded by tiny droplets of blood and red patches of skin. The witch's lips were pulled into a thin line, deepening the wrinkles around her mouth. "Not quite, Finley. Finish the job."

Finley let out another grunt, leaning on one hand against a thigh. "You could at least admire the work. You think that's easy, even for a Gnome? That's real art."

Lizzie let her arm hang in the air, waiting him out. Her other hand was resting easily against her wand that was tucked in the long pocket specially sewn into her pants.

"Fine, I get it. You're a badass now." He whispered quietly under his breath, sucking in air. "Restore, relax, rejuvenate," he said, and slowly let out a breath that shimmered in the light. The air passed over Lizzie's arm dropping silvery particles as it passed the wound, melting into the skin. The redness passed, receding toward the tattoo till it vanished altogether. The droplets of blood that remained began to vibrate, shrinking in size with each jiggle till they were gone as well. Lizzie started to lean forward but Finley held up his hand, not looking up from her wrist. "Patience," he said in a low growl.

Seconds went by and finally, a silver mist began to rise from her wrist, the eerie fog climbing up her arm and jumping to her chest. The witch sat back hard against the chair, her eyes open in surprise as she tried to catch her breath. She gulped in small breaths as her skin turned from a honey color to a silvery gray. Her mouth opened wide, even as she tried to shut it, the silver mist flooding out the opening, leaving her body.

"Didn't anybody warn you?" asked an incredulous Finley, scratching the back of his head.

Lizzie tried to shake her head, but she was pinned against the chair as the mist continued to roll out into the open space, immediately dissolving and disappearing. Finally, her jaw relaxed and she snapped her mouth shut, holding very still. A tear rolled down her cheek. "The essence is gone," she whispered. "Forty years, just like that."

"Of course it is. Leaves kind of an odor, don't you think?" The Gnome sniffed the air. "There is no longer a trace of the Silver Griffins left in you. You are unbound."

Finley rolled forward and examined the wrist again, holding it up for Lizzie to see. "Happy now?" He was still looking for a little praise.

Lizzie held her hand closer, splaying her fingers as she moved her wrist around, trying to catch the tattoo in just the right light. She glanced up at Finley. "You do good work, and you know it."

Finley snorted with delight and held out his meaty hand. Lizzie dropped the gold coins into his palm, watching them disappear into his fist. The Gnome sat back in his swivel chair, rolling just far enough out of the light. "You sure you know what you're doing? I mean, I get it. Silver Griffins. Poof!" He blew air out his cheeks in the shadows, letting his fingers dance through the air. "Betrayed by your own kind --"

"Scattered like pebbles, the vault destroyed, hunted like stray dogs." Lizzie smacked her lips together to get rid of the bitter taste. "It's time we fought back, by any means necessary. Someone has to."

"Yeah, but don't you think the head witch, what's her name?"

"Lois? No, I don't!" snapped Lizzie. "It's been months and nothing. No word, no help, nothing done to stop all the killings." Lizzie thrust out her arm, pulling up her sleeve even higher to reveal a burn mark that was still healing. "Elf magic. I barely survived the ambush." Her eyes shone with tears. "I was the only survivor," she said quietly, letting her arm fall into her lap. Another tear rolled down her cheek.

"Okay, okay." Finley held up his hands in protest. "I get it. I suppose I'd do the same if it was my brethren. Hell, we'd have already amassed an army and come in, axes swinging. Maybe bring something that breathes fire." He snorted loudly, stomping his large boot.

Lizzie slowly stood up. "Time to get on with things. Join the others."

"There must be hundreds of you by now. Anyone got an actual plan?" Finley gently picked up the tattoo machine and stood up, lumbering to his full height. He was more wide than tall.

The aging witch took out her wand and circled it around her head, startled at the appearance of a fine red dust falling around her.

"That's new." Finley smiled again, putting out his hand to let the dust fall on the tips of his calloused fingers.

Lizzie felt a catch in her chest. "Did I do the right thing?" she muttered, still turning the wand in a slow circle. But the images of her friends being sliced open with razor sharp bolts of magic haunted her. Romley, a young wizard about to get married, Penny, a witch with twenty years service and Wombley, a wizard who was accustomed to working in the vault, never seeing any action. "Wombley." Lizzie gently pressed her hand against her chest.

They had all dropped behind her as she turned to help. "Too, too late," she whispered. Wombley looked so surprised as he stared up at Lizzie. His brows were knit together just like they did when he couldn't quite figure out where to place an item in the vault.

The memory of watching the light fade and then the flash of silver leave his body when he finally died wouldn't leave her alone. "I got away." The red dust continued to fall around her, coloring her shoulders. She had squeezed through a narrow portal in the nick of time, leaving the burn mark on her arm.

"Time to do something," she said, the fine red powder

dusting her lips. Lizzie lifted her chin and wiped her eyes on her sleeve. "I lived so I could hunt their killers. Enough already. This is a new day."

"So, no plan." Finley shook his head. "Everything needs a plan. You think I'm gonna try a tattoo with no plan? Sign of an amateur." He pointed a stubby finger at Lizzie. "And you're no amateur. You know better!"

"We have our own lists," growled Lizzie, still angry from the memories. It was how her days went lately. Sadness to anger and back again. "All of us kept lists. Every Silver Griffin had documentation they kept for themselves." Her voice was rising to a shout. "It made it easier to know who were the bad players in our areas and faster to find them." She spit out the words, baring her teeth. "Magical filth, every one of them. Trevilsom Prison is too good for them."

"That is saying something." A shudder passed through the muscular Gnome, shaking his body. "I had a cousin get out of there. Never the same."

Lizzie blinked, spinning her wand faster. "We have a plan. To wipe away their existence. No one will stop us."

"Not even the Fixer? He'll catch on to what you're doing. And I've heard stories about his mate. What is her name?" He tapped the side of his head, squinting. "Leira?"

"No one," Lizzie barked.

The red dust swirled around her, faster and faster till she disappeared from the room.

"Whatever you say," said Finley, watching fascinated as the red dust gathered in a pile, dancing along the floor, swirling up into a cloud and vanishing with a loud clap.

## CHAPTER ELEVEN

Leira slipped her right arm into her leather jacket, not sure where to start. She looked down at her left arm, the symbols picking up speed, and saw the pattern. "Wait, what? How is that possible?" Her grandmother's name scrolled along her arm, written in ancient symbols. *Mara Berens.* She slipped her other arm into the jacket and looked up at the ceiling of her bedroom, weighing the odds of her grandmother being involved. "Mara? Not a chance in hell. Not this time, anyway. Mara would never leave the school unattended to find revenge."

The old scar on her side twitched, sending a ping of sharp pain all the way back to her spine. "Fuck me," said the bounty hunter, leaning over slightly, massaging her belly. "First Perrom, now you?"

"Maybe." Yumfuck stood in the doorway. "Maybe. Maybe Mara has done something," he said with a shrug. "I'll still have her back. It's what friends do." He held up his paw. "But she's not the revenge type. Not on a large scale." He wrinkled his nose, waving a paw. "Ah, the dead fish stare, a classic," he said, patting his chest gently. "I miss Hagan too."

Leira ignored the comment, feeling a pang for her old partner anyway. "This is different, Yumfuck. It's her friends who are dying and we're not at the end, yet. It's exactly the kind of thing she would do."

Yumfuck ran to the bed and nimbly climbed up the bed post, digging his claws into the wooden post. There were scores of previous, tiny holes already laid out like straight train tracks up to the rounded knob.

The troll stood on top, balancing neatly on his paw, stretching up to his full six inches. "Don't sell your grandmother short. Not that fast at least. She would do something, but it would be the right thing, *leaning* on the rules. Not busting through them."

Leira kicked off her running shoes. Her favorite attire. She stopped with her hands on her hips to look at Yumfuck. The symbols on her arms were spinning faster. Something was playing itself out, building to a crescendo. "You have a point. If anyone could find a way to stay just within the lines, it's a Berens. I have to go."

She got down on her hands and knees and pulled out the tall, brown leather boots that were a little lighter color than her jacket, and with steel in the toes. It didn't hurt that Correk had put a spell over them without telling Leira. Still, she had known the moment she saw them, watching the magic twirl around the heels. He was always looking for small ways to protect her without getting in the way.

The memory could still make her smile even in the midst of turmoil. Like now.

Suddenly, a wisp of energy wrapped around her waist,

warming her torso and rising up her chest to her throat, turning the skin a rosy pink. "Mara," she whispered.

*Hurry.*

Leira heard the plea clear as a bell without anyone saying anything. Her eyes widened, glowing and she glanced at Yumfuck, even as she was opening a portal, letting the magic guide her.

But Yumfuck took her hand at the last second, grasping her finger and making her pause. "The scales are tipped in the wrong direction right now. Remember that and fight accordingly. Pull back if you need to and go back another day. I know, I know," he said, shaking his furry green head. "It's not in your nature. But these times will require you to always remember the bigger picture. If we are to win the war, we must lose some battles. It will never matter how many times you put your enemy down. Only that they stay there. And you have not seen an enemy like this before." He let go of her hand as she pulled away, stepping quickly through the portal while glancing back at the troll with a furrowed brow.

"Remember," he squeaked, still balancing on the bed.

---

The troll sat on the newel of the staircase in front of the door wearing his tiny cowboy hat and blue boots. He was holding Leira's phone. Yumfuck had conveniently slipped it off the kitchen table when she went upstairs, distracted.

"Not my first rodeo," he said, hitting send. "Yeehaw, motherfuckers! Come on Grub Hub. Time to eat my feelings."

Occasionally the fur along his back stood on end and he sat up, ready to go to Leira, watching the color of his fur for any changes. But just as quickly the hair would settle back down and he would lean back, scrolling through menus. Uber Eats was already on their way.

"Next up, Door Dash! Dessert, dessert, dessert," he muttered, looking through the menus. "Yeah, the creme brulee. Ooooh, a little cheese flan. Yes, please. Ya, I *will* take a torte. Thank you very munch, munch, munch. *Send.*" He smacked his lips, licking his tiny teeth when he was jolted upright. The phone fell from his hand, hitting the bottom stair and flipping over to the floor.

"Leira? You okay?" The troll looked from side to side, waiting, the first tremor going down his back, and moving back and forth. "Time to go," he shouted, throwing off the hat and boots. He traced the air in front of him with a sharp nail, cutting a hole till there was the beginning of a portal and pushing outward till the flap bent in to make a tunnel to another place. "Leira, I'm coming!" he shouted, diving forward and rolling to the grassy ground on the other side. He stood up, already growing to his full eight-foot height, growling and slashing at the air.

Yumfuck sniffed the air and picked up the scent of Leira's magic that was always connected to him. Ashy smoke was blended into it along with a sense of urgency.

"I'm coming," he yelled in his deep rumble, running quickly across the Virginia countryside toward the School of Necessary Magic only a few miles away. He could see the thin spire of smoke just above the treetops. "No!" The troll lifted his chin and let out a roar that echoed through the trees, even as he picked up the pace.

The delivery man walked away from the house, smiling back at Correk who was standing in the foyer holding three large orders, frowning and confused. He shut the front door, distracted by his sore shoulder. "Yumfuck!" he yelled up the stairs, lifting the bags to smell each one. "If you're not down here in the next minute I'm going to start licking everything." Correk shook his head. "That won't slow him down," he muttered.

"Yumfuck?" he bellowed, looking up the stairs and hesitating, listening for scratching, rustling, crawling. Something.

He opened the bag, breathing in the smell of onion rings. "Serves him right," he said. He looked up the stairs again, listening for any sounds of movement. Nothing. "Eating. I'm going to start eating. Working my way through whatever has the most grease and sugar," he yelled. The house was quiet.

His brow furrowed and he went to set the bags down by the stairs, ready to take the steps two at a time. A troll was always ready to defend fast food. "Especially this troll." He stepped around the bags. "Are you sick?" Correk's voice softened as his foot kicked something.

He looked down and quickly knelt, picking up Leira's forgotten phone. His eyes widened and he squeezed the phone in his hand, willing it to tell him something but there was no magic residue. Only the troll's greasy fingerprints. He cocked his head to one side, listening to the magic stream that was always flowing around him for any signs of trouble. Once he filtered out the constant chatter from magicals he detected a distant echo, but he couldn't be sure where it was coming from or who was sending it. Still, he knew it was trouble.

"Something powerful is blocking me." He gently shook his head. There was a familiar taint to the energy in his way, but he couldn't quite place it. A tightness grew in his chest. "Leira, where are you?" He forced himself to take a deep breath and remember what Turner Underwood had taught him.

*In the darkest moments, pause and listen to the undercurrent of magic all around you. It will never fail you.*

The Light Elf let the breath out slowly, whispering an ancient spell known only to Fixers through the generations. "I am one with all things. Mother of all Worlds, Father of all Skies, connected to all things. Everything is known." He relaxed, surrendering to the magic surging through his veins and pounding in his head.

*This is what separates all magicals from Fixers*, Turner had said. *Anyone can say the spell, but can you surrender to it? Surrender everything and believe its simple truth? That is what makes you a Fixer among magicals. Trust in the magic.*

Correk felt the temptation to move faster, look for Leira's deep purple trail but he resisted, feeling his way into the magic gathering around him. "Trust," he whispered, holding the phone more gently. "Trust everything."

Slowly his view of the front hall changed, bands of shimmering colors rising up from the floor. The colors quickly separated themselves into tiny balls of bright, piercing light, reforming into a portal. Where there were once stairs and a hallway to the kitchen there was now an open doorway to a rolling green field and trees. Correk lifted his chin, feeling the dread that was wafting in from the portal. A nearby battle.

The smell of smoke quickly filled the front hall and the distant smoke was making the faraway landscape hazy.

The new Fixer didn't hesitate, taking two long strides into the portal, his eyes scanning the horizon till he saw the smoke above the trees and could finally recognize the area. "The school." His heart pounded as he began to run, searching the ground for signs of Leira or even the troll.

It wasn't long before he picked up both trails, the deep purple already fading while the lime green of the troll was still vibrant and pulsating. *Not together. Yumfuck got here later.*

He tried opening another portal to help him cross the miles more quickly but there was the same odor and another shove from someone else's magic. He pushed through the dense woods that surrounded the school, bending back thin branches and quickly ducking under bigger ones, the muscles along his back rippling from the effort.

A rattlesnake crept out from its hiding place under an old log, hissing at Correk and rattling its tail. Correk turned two fingers in a semi-circle, pacifying the snake, even as he kept feeling for signs of distress. Faint cries from Witches and Wizards reached him, all coming from the same direction. Straight ahead. He picked up his pace, creating a path among the trees where there wasn't one. Scratches appeared on his arms from the sharp branches, quickly repairing themselves, but he didn't take note.

There was only one thought. *Who is after Leira?* The

faint stench of something dark and magical was there again. "No," he said, biting off the word.

He broke through the other side of the forest, coming out onto the road that encircled the school, just in front of the tall iron gate. A portion of the fence was badly damaged, several of the stout metal stakes bent down toward the ground. A crisscross pattern of different magical trails covered the area. None of them were Leira or the troll.

Correk quickly looked to the left and right for any other signs of destruction. *Nothing.*

He easily crawled over the bent spikes and kept moving toward the smoke, crossing the playing fields, and moving around the old barns. There was no sign of the grounds keeper, Horace Rigby, and the horses were kicking at the doors to their stalls, braying loudly.

Correk began running, making his way to the main hall and the source of the smoke. At last, he could hear the commotion. He rounded the far corner of the large, stately building and saw her. Leira with her arms out and the troll towering over her. They were standing side by side with their backs to Correk.

In front of them were a row of magicals stepping through the veil from the World in Between, mired in the Dark Mist. The black goo was clinging to their legs, pushing them forward. Correk started, recognizing some of their faces. "All dead," he muttered, the energy inside his body burning at the edges, swirling in a sour pool in the center of his gut, pushing at his ribs. He moved more slowly toward Leira, taking in the blank, dark eyes of the encroaching departed. The Dark Mist was flowing out ahead of them, reaching toward Leira even as Yumfuck growled and slashed at the creeping tide.

"Leira," he said evenly, taking her hand as he took his place beside her.

"Correk," she said in a whisper, turning to glance at him before looking quickly back at the approaching menace. "A sickly new twist." She held up her hand, letting a white fireball grow in her hand. Jasper magic. She slowly let the ball roll out of her hand toward the Dark Mist, burning the edges and creating a foul, rotting odor. The fiery ball eventually reached one of the combatants, rolling up his leg as he moaned, turning him into ash. The gray flecks floated down to the Dark Mist, quickly reabsorbed, vanishing beneath the surface.

"That will get me to sleep with the light on for a while." Leira opened her hand, letting another ball form. "Something I learned from Tess. Work with the magic, not against it. Energy is always looking for balance. The Dark Mist is only half of the balance, always seeking the light." She let the ball roll out of her fingers. "Let's give it some more of the other half and see what happens."

A dead magical lunged toward Yumfuck, their grey hands reaching for the troll's fur. Yumfuck roared and swung a large paw down in a curve, taking off the late wizard's head. Black ooze seeped out of the neck. The body helplessly wandered back and forth as the head bobbed on the surface of the Dark Mist.

Leira's eyes grew wider, even as the fireball sought out another target.

Yumfuck stayed by Leira's side, his razor-sharp claws

slicing through anyone that got too close to her. His claws were covered in the sticky, black remains.

It wasn't long before tendrils of inky, black liquid thinned out enough to slide up what remained of the fallen bodies and a small wave rose up over any floating heads, engulfing the pieces. The remains of a tall, angular wizard were the last to be pulled under even as his arms tried to claw at the liquid that was consuming him, yet again. The ones left standing stepped through the area unimpeded, marching closer. Their eyes were shiny reflections of black.

Finally, the blazing white fireball came to rest in the center of the space between Leira and the ghoulish menace. Leira's eyes began to glow and the symbols on her arms picked up speed, announcing something new. She held out her hands, twisting them one way, and then another as the energy surged up her legs all the way to her neck.

Her body began to vibrate, giving off a low hum that was barely audible. Correk reached out to touch her. "What are you doing? Let me ground you," he barked.

"No! I'm okay. I'm working with it. You have to trust me." She glanced at him, looking into his eyes. "Trust me," she said, turning back to face the Dark Mist. She spread her fingers wide and held herself steady, letting the magic go out ahead of her, seeking out the fireball resting on the surface of the Dark Mist, waiting for her instructions.

The Jasper Elf let out a short grunt as her magic made contact, her head rocking back just a little. Her eyes flickered left and right as she watched the fireball expand, spreading its light across the surface of the Dark Mist, bonding with the thick mass. *Let the magic do its work.* Leira slowly took in a breath, resisting the urge to hurry.

The light skipped across the surface, skating just above the Dark Mist, spreading around the dead magicals sending an eerie, warm reflection up their bodies and under their chins, highlighting their gaunt features. The bright fireball slowly flattened out, even as the illumination increased, drawing energy from the Dark Mist.

Correk shielded his eyes, watching in amazement. "It's working," he said, as the Dark Mist shuddered in a wide ripple. The entire gelatinous tide rolled toward Leira in one last effort and then rolled back, large bubbles rising up through the white glare, breaking open and emitting a steamy gas. "That fish smell." Correk choked out the words. "There it is again."

"It's not the Dark Mist." Leira kept her arms outstretched, holding the light steady as it clung to her old foe. "Something is buried inside of it. I can feel it. My energy is bonding with it and I can feel what it's feeling."

"That thing does not feel." The muscles in Correk's cheek worked as he clenched his teeth.

"It kind of does. It has to have a million souls wrapped up in it. Thousands of years of swallowing magicals. They're all there, twisted into one creepy fucking mind."

"Wolfstan."

"There's no sign of him. None. I can't feel him among the dead."

*Flash!*

A phosphorescent bang of light cracked along the surface of the Dark Mist. The dead witches and wizards, gnomes and dwarves in front of them startled, their mouths in a collective gape.

"What in the name of fucking hell?" Leira's body ached from the effort of the energy running through her, but she held her stance. "No one deserves that ending," she muttered. "Except maybe Wolfstan."

The Dark Mist had almost reached Leira's feet when it suddenly stopped. The dark tide rose up, poking holes in places through the bright light, suddenly tugging at the waist of each of them, pulling them smoothly back under the surface even as their arms flailed through the air in protest. Black droplets remained, sparkling against the gleam of the light still embedded on top of it.

Leira curved her back into a C-shape, recoiling from the feeling of something punching her in the stomach. She sipped at the air, pressing her hand against her belly, blinking hard against the nausea.

"Are you alright?" Correk grasped Leira tightly at the elbow, looking back over his shoulder at the receding tide. "What made it give up? What was buried in there?"

Leira willed herself to stand up straight. "Relax," she muttered, remembering one of Turner Underwood's first lessons. *When the urge to pull away shows itself, lean in harder.*

Her eyes were still aglow and even though the Dark Mist was nowhere to be seen anymore, the symbols along her arms were still spinning, sending out future calculations, weighing the odds. Leira took in a deep breath and held it, letting it out slowly, opening her arms wide.

"What are you doing?" Correk reluctantly let go of her arm, watching the symbols flip over and over. "No, Leira, no! You gave your word."

The troll roared in response, throwing his head back and beating his chest with his large paws.

"It's not what you think," said Leira, "I'm letting the magic go out ahead of me to follow the trail. I'm secure here." She felt the ache in her chest. *Was that a lie?* "Something is different, can't you feel it? That ocean of misery has changed, morphed." The Jasper Elf let out another breath, letting go of trying to control the energy inside of her. *Show me.*

"We need to check on Mara." Correk looked over his shoulder again toward the main building.

His voice was an echo to her. Leira was riding along the top of the magic, watching it curl around the traces of the Dark Mist, careful not to come into contact. "There," she blurted in surprise, watching the energy skip toward a portal that was no more than a slit, no wider than a mail slot, hanging in the air. "The World in Between," she said. Her magic stopped just short of the rip connecting the two worlds. Leira watched in awe, her eyes widening in surprise. "Fuck me, of course there is a tear."

Just on the other side of the hole, the black goo of the Dark Mist was streaming past as if it were a rushing river, pulsating with an eerie, steady beat of glittering black, gelatinous slime.

"Where is it?" Correk put his hand on Leira's shoulder, but her magic resisted the connection, pushing him away at first. "Remember, you're more than a Jasper Elf, Leira. Let the spark show me what you see."

Leira felt the shift inside her chest. The spark of humanity was starting to roil and pop, seeking out the request to bond, fulfilling its nature.

The muscles in Correk's chest and face tightened, creating an uncomfortable pressure against the force of energy pushing at him. It was the first time he had ever felt the full strength of Leira's power pass through him. Yumfuck's trail of sparkling green passed easily by him, entwining Leira's energy.

Correk gripped Leira's shoulder tighter, looking around in amazement, surrounded by her magic. "Not even Turner--" He turned his head slowly from side to side, bracing his legs. The magic intensified even further, reluctantly welcoming the extra rider and enveloping the Light Elf in its power. His feet slid backward a few inches and he grunted from the strain. But he managed to lean forward, falling deeper into the stream of magic.

It felt as if Leira's magic could lift him off the ground.

He felt the muscles along his back twitch from the effort, even as he was distracted by something else. Mixed inside of the stream was something else he'd never seen before, never heard Turner mention. He felt himself drawn toward it, stepping through the thin, golden flow, suddenly drenched in the love Leira carried for him, buried deep inside of her.

Somewhere, underneath that was the piece she held back, even from herself.

Memories of her childhood flooded through him. Her mother being taken away. Mara missing for so long. The years of silently living behind Estelle's bar.

"All the loss," he whispered, finally sharing the pain she tucked away all the time. He reached out his hand instinctively, wanting to heal the wound. "That's what the Dark Mist feels in you. It's not just the light." Leira didn't look at him, keeping her face turned toward the path. "Okay, not now, but soon," he said. He gently slid his hand up the back of her neck, pressing it against her skin. A hum passed through his fingers, the loneliness she carried passing through his bones. "I didn't know," he whispered.

He heard the familiar tap-tap against the hard ground and felt the faint chill in the air that only another Fixer would detect.

"Neither does she." Turner Underwood doffed his bowler in a roll down his arm, catching it neatly in one hand. The other hand was leaning on the silver knob of his cane. He was standing in the middle of a deep fog that was encircling Correk. The old Fixer pressed a finger to his lips. "Our fierce warrior doesn't know I'm here. Best she focus on the mission in front of her. Facing our demons can be a distraction."

"You knew?" Correk kept his hand resting against his mate. "Why didn't you help her?"

Turner shrugged. "Some things we have to discover for ourselves. Otherwise, it's just words." He tapped the cane against the ground again, scattering what remained of the Dark Mist's presence. "Both of you have seen enough. Go where you're needed. Tend to Mara. Remember? This can wait." He held up a large, aging hand. "It can wait," he said firmly. "Enough revelations for one afternoon. Go, young Fixer."

"I'm over a hundred years old."

"A young lad." Turner put his hat back on his head and

tapped the top lightly with the tip of his fingers, disappearing in a cloud of mist that faded away.

Correk startled, his attention turning back to Leira. He felt her letting go of the surge of energy within her body, watching it spiral back toward her and down through her legs, back into the ground. His heart was still pounding from the effort of blending with her energy.

Her face turned up, gazing at him with her eyes still glowing. He looked down at her in wonder.

"We need to go," she said, glancing down at her arm. "Mara's still in trouble." She grasped Correk's hand, squeezing it tight. "Ready?"

Yumfuck stood behind her, towering over her, making low grunts and angry grumbles. His paws tore at the air over Leira's head as she took off at a run. The troll didn't hesitate, quickly following behind her.

"Trust the magic," he muttered. He began to run, his long legs helping him to catch up to the pair, taking his place on the other side of Leira. It wasn't long before they arrived at the main hall and the grand entrance. The heavy wooden doors were hanging off their hinges, deep claw marks across one side. Leira's brow furrowed. "Trolls?"

Yumfuck shook his head in disgust. "Never. Kilomea warriors. Hired help." He drove a fist against the door, splintering the deepest scratches and pointing out three cross hatches in a vertical line. "Their calling card." The troll ran for the stairs without waiting for anyone, dropping to all four paws to move even faster, baring his teeth. The green hair on his head stood up straight, bristling with anger.

"Wait!" Leira caught up to the troll at the top of the stairs, pushing past him. He gave way, making room for her but stayed only one step away from Leira, moving swiftly up the stairs behind her.

Leira could feel the familiar energy of her grandmother nearby. She reached out her hand, the fingers spread wide letting the magic act like a compass. A warmth caressed the end of her fingertips pulling her hand to the left. "This way."

The trio ran down the wide hallway to the left, coming to the old classroom dedicated to magic history. Leira stopped short, the pungent smell of wet Kilomea fur wafting out to her. She paused, letting Correk catch up and opened her hand, looking at him as small, white-hot fireballs formed in her hand. He nodded and pulled out the longer of the two knives he always had with him.

Leira hesitated a moment longer, taking a deep breath and letting her magic reach out for help. It wasn't long before Eireka Berens' gentle magic wrapped itself around Leira, seeking out the trouble. "Mom," Leira whispered, pressing the heel of her palm against her chest. Her mother's energy pressed softly against her, urging her forward.

She threw the fireballs at an angle into the open room, even as her mother's energy passed through her, seeking out Mara Berens, creating a bridge between all three women.

Just as quickly as the miniature fireballs were released, more appeared in her hand, skipping out across the floor, seeking out their targets. The acrid smell of burning fur quickly replaced the musty odor followed by angry, guttural screams. "Now!" yelled Leira, pushing into the classroom.

Mara and an older professor with a gray beard and dark glasses were standing shoulder to shoulder in front of five teenage students with their wands raised, ready to fight. "Leira! I knew you would come." A wash of relief passed over Mara's face even as she kept her wand raised and her other arm outstretched to hold back the eager students. Two large Kilomeas stood in front of them, their fur still burning. Leira threw out another handful of the small firebrands, even as her mother's energy guided the white-hot missiles to encircle the Kilomeas legs, crawling up their large bodies.

Yumfuck came into the room, easily matching their size and took advantage of the distraction, slashing at the throat of the closest Kilomea, easily opening a large vein. The large beast dropped to his knees, his paws grasping fruitlessly at the gaping wound.

The other Kilomea was busy stomping out the remaining fireballs with his leathery foot, weapons arranged across his chest, hooked to crossed cloth straps. He roared in anger and frustration.

"The day is not with you," shouted Correk, sliding around till he was in front of Mara and the others.

The Kilomea curled his lip and took a step toward Correk but the Light Elf was faster, slicing through the air with the long knife, slashing the top of the beast's hand. The professor followed up with a spell. "The ties that bind!" A bronze rope lined with thorns emerged from his wand, winding itself around the Kilomea, digging into his skin.

The Kilomea cried out and stepped back again, faltering, fighting his way out of the rope.

"You're outnumbered. Go or meet the same fate as your buddy." Mara raised her wand, ready to start a spell.

It only took the Kilomea a moment to come up with an alternate plan, crashing through the second-floor window and dropping to the ground below. Leira ran to the window and looked down, watching him nimbly stand and shake it off. He looked up at the broken window and gave out a last angry roar before running for the nearby woods.

Mara joined Leira at the window. "He's probably got a portal back to Oriceran open by now. I don't think he expected so much resistance." Leira's grandmother looked back at the dead Kilomea sprawled on the old wooden floors. "The opposition has branched out."

"Was this all of them? They did all this destruction?"

"Oh no, there were a few Gnomes and Wizards and Witches mixed in with these two brutes. The other professors were able to dispatch them one way or another. Not the brightest bunch. These two, though, were another story. Brawn and brains with weapons. I was a little worried."

The professor wiped his forehead with the back of his hand. "I think I sweated through my jacket."

Mara smiled and patted the professor gently on the back, making Leira take a second look. "Leira, meet Professor Xander Powell, the Dark Energy teacher. Professor Powell, this is my granddaughter, Leira Berens. The tall drink of water is her Elf partner in all things, Correk. And of course, Yumfuck Tiberius Troll--"

Yumfuck lumbered over, swooping Mara into his large,

furry arms and holding her off the ground, squeezing tight. He let out a mournful cry, howling with his head tilted back.

"Okay, okay," said Mara, patting the troll on his back. "I'm alright. You can put me down. Quit shaking me or I'll drop my lucky cards." Yumfuck gently put her down, letting out another cry.

"Yumfuck, it's okay." Leira knelt and held out her hand close to the ground. "Come on, it's time. The danger has passed. You can stand down." The troll shuddered, taking a long look around before shrinking down to only six inches tall and jumping into Leira's hand. She scooped up her bonded friend and dropped him into her coat pocket. The teenagers crowded around her, clamoring to see the small troll. Yumfuck peered back out of the pocket, smiling and chirping. "Aloha motherfuckers!"

Mara rolled her eyes. "I suppose I can take credit for that one." She shrugged, shaking her head. "That should be good for a few angry emails." She smiled and winked at the students. "How about we don't repeat that phrase? Go on, get down to the dining hall and see if you can help with the clean-up. There's a lot to do. Go on!"

She pushed them toward the door, leaning around the corner to make sure they kept going down the hall toward the stairs. "Now then," said Mara, coming to the center of the room, letting out a deep breath. "We need to talk. This has gone on long enough. Either of you two have a plan?"

Leira noted the smile that appeared and faded in a moment on Professor Powell's face. "No, but I have plenty of questions," she said, still looking between the two of them.

"That's as good a place as any to start," said her grandmother.

"How about we start with what the Dark Mist was doing in your backyard?"

"That is a separate issue, my dear. Start by asking why those who wanted to finish off the Silver Griffins were willing to hire hairy mercenaries that are hard to control under the best conditions."

Leira shook her head in frustration but knew better than to push her grandmother too hard. She could sense Mara's resolve. "Okay, I'll bite. What do you have on them?"

"There you go. A much better question. I have a combined list of known whereabouts of most of them. We've been using it to help agents steer clear. I'm afraid someone on the inside may have ratted me out."

"Motherfuckers," chirped Yumfuck, leaning out of Leira's pocket and shaking his fist.

"What he said." Leira arched a brow, her hands in fists, propped on her hips. "You could have shared the list with me, you know."

"Not till I had to. We needed them to be in the dark and my granddaughter rounding them up would have given them a heads up. You're kind of a well known bounty hunter in their circles." Mara threw up her hands. "No point now. Someone has told on us. The list is quickly becoming useless."

"I may be able to help find out more," said Professor Powell. "I still have friends in low places."

"I'll go with you," said Correk, surprising Leira, but she said nothing, squeezing his hand.

The professor hesitated but finally gave a nod. "I suppose a Fixer is always an ice breaker."

Correk kissed the top of Leira's head before leaning down to put his forehead to hers. "I will see you at home and we will talk. About everything." He kissed the top of her head again, putting an arm around her shoulders. "The coordinates, Professor? I can open a portal."

Professor Powell swirled his wand in the air, the numbers making a neat circle becoming a jumbled ball before finding their place, mapping out the destination. Correk snapped his fingers, opening a portal in the middle of the room.

"That is a very clever Elf," said Mara.

On the other side of the portal was a narrow cobble stoned street between brick buildings. "Philadelphia," said the professor. "After you."

Correk squeezed Leira's hand and let go, giving her a brief smile before nudging her pocket. Yumfuck poked out his head, rubbing his face. "Look after her," whispered Correk. "Always," said the troll, disappearing back into the pocket. Correk rubbed his hand against Leira's cheek and turned to go through the portal. "I'll be back by nightfall," he said, as the professor followed behind him and the portal began to close.

"That was odd," said Mara, as the room returned to a quiet classroom. "Does he always act like the worst is yet to come?"

"Grandma, this is all odd and has been for years. There's a dead beast on the floor and a large broken window where the other one got away. And the Dark Mist paid you a visit.

Point out the normal parts." Leira pressed her palms to her forehead.

"This is the School of Necessary Magic. The occasional misunderstanding is to be expected."

Leira gave a short laugh. "They practically burned down your school. Never mind, I get it. Let go and move on, as quickly as possible. Otherwise, it's all too much. Isn't that what you told me once?"

Mara smiled, satisfied and turned to go.

"Not so fast," said Leira. "The Dark Mist. Why here? You know something." Leira's eyes took on a faint glow.

Mara turned back and pressed her lips together, taking a beat. "It's not good news, but I suppose you should know. That slime, whatever it is, seemed to predict your visit. Like it knew you would be arriving and set a trap."

"You called me here. Of course I came." Leira noticed the momentary startle come across her grandmother. "No," she whispered. "That's not possible. It was your magic. I'm sure of it."

"No, dear," said Mara, her eyes growing wider. "It wasn't. Damn it."

Leira took a deep breath and held it for a moment, letting it out slowly. "Fuck me. It knew just how to get me here. How will I know when it's really you or not? I'll have to be ready for anything, every time."

"That's sage advice, no matter what." Mara tapped the side of her nose. "But don't give in so easily. You are a Jasper Elf with a side of a spark of humanity. Next time you feel a connection to me, or Eireka, or even your father, take a moment. Let the magic go out ahead of you and check on things. You'll know the difference no matter what the darkness brings. Love can't be imitated. Use all of your being to detect the truth." Mara hugged her granddaughter.

Leira relaxed in her arms, feeling Mara's magic blend in with her mother's that was still connecting the three women. Two tiny furry little paws came out of Leira's pocket, pressing against Leira as well.

Even as she let herself be enveloped by the warmth of their magic, there was one thought that danced in her head. *Something is wrong.* A shudder passed through her, but she shook it off, pulling back. "Show me the list. Not all of them will have changed places. Time to fill Trevilsom Prison."

## CHAPTER TWELVE

The Dark Gardener leaned forward on the horned lion, standing in the stirrups, raising the long, heavy carved club over his head as he rode through the Dark Forest. Trees bent out of the way and deer with feathered antlers leapt over dead stumps, disappearing into the deeper woods.

The Gardener was making his way through the forest, creating a grid of his own making. There were signs of intruders into the protected woods just outside of Austin, Texas. An underground burrow of black cats with long, peacock tails was caved in on the side. The feral cats with their long, wide blue and green feathered tails were nowhere to be seen. The rare animals were known for their ability to track even the smallest creatures and were highly prized as helpers by hunters on Oriceran. But no Elf, no Gnome or Dwarf, or even Kilomea would dare to steal one from a protected forest. Tales of the Gardener's revenge were legendary, even if all the stories weren't true.

There were no signs of animal tracks, no nearby

crushed twigs and nothing else was out of place. Only the faint remnants of a magical trail that seemed to go nowhere, disappearing into the ground.

Further into the interior, the Gardener pulled back on the reins, slowing the lion. A small copse of trees were cut down to pointed stumps, creating a circle that pointed to an open space in the canopy overhead. The Gardener looked up, studying the sky but there was nothing. Only the occasional cry of a spider monkey or the sound of songbirds fluttering from one tree to the next.

The Gardener sat back, his hand holding tight to the reins, sitting very still, even as the vines in his hair wound their way in and out of his long, dark locks. He was aware of every sound that passed through the forest and could peel back the layers, listening for what didn't belong. There was nothing.

He sat back, loosening his hold and gave a gentle nudge to the lion's ribs, motioning him slowly forward. The lion was used to moving through the woods without a sound as he crept forward, slowly picking up speed. The Gardener's pointed ears twitched, turning slightly, but still nothing.

The lion saw it first, stopping suddenly and letting out a low growl. The Gardener saw the scratches in the old elm tree and felt a chill pass through him. An outline of a severed hand was burned into the wood and traces of black ooze filled in the crevices of the bark all around it.

The Gardener slipped off the lion and crouched by the symbol, dipping his fingers into the dark goo and smelling the remains. The damp, musty odor that always reminded him of the dead clung to it. But there was something else.

An acrid, bitter sliver of magic that wound its way through the slime, leaving behind a trail of hardened crystals.

"Wolfstan." The Gardener bit off the word, spitting it out in a quiet anger. He stood, placing a hand on the lion's neck, the coarse, wavy yellow hair of the mane covering his fingers. He pounded the ground with the bottom of his staff, shaking the ground for miles. Every creature in the forest knew the warning. Take cover, stay low to the ground, or high in the trees. Be quiet and wait for the danger to pass. Something wicked walks this way, threatening the safety of the entire forest.

---

Wolfstan Humphrey slid out of the Dark Mist, the black tide clinging to the heels of his boots. His right arm ended in a stump at the wrist, crisscrossed with dark, ropey red scars.

Most of the thoughts in his head were a jumble, giving him a general, dull headache. But there was one idea that stood out, clear as a bell. *I will have my revenge, on everyone. No matter the cost.*

He stood in the corner of the World in Between near the tear that the Dark Mist guarded, waiting somewhat patiently for the twisted energy that ruled the vast space.

They had a deal after all.

It was an easy transition for him, once he found the opening and crawled through, escaping the bloody battlefield. The memory of the battle, what was supposed to be his victory, made him tremble with rage. "Damn Jasper Elf." He waved his remaining fist in the air.

It wasn't long after his arrival that the darkness that crept through the World in Between sought him out. He didn't resist, sensing an opportunity, even as he watched others who were trapped there, the living and the dead, scurrying to get away. Perhaps there was a deal to be made.

"Surely you must want something?" he had asked the darkness as it slid closer to him. A wall of dark energy had pulsed around him, trying to make sense of this new entity that had willingly crawled into its midst.

He had felt the sudden electrical sparks riding along the surface of his skin, singeing the hairs. He winced in pain, glancing over his shoulder at the entrance the Dark Mist was protecting. But Wolfstan believed everyone and everything in this world, and the next, wanted something and he had the fool's optimism that made him think he could get it for them. In exchange for a favor, of course.

*Here it comes.*

He felt the sense of dread that came over the World in Between when the darkness was on the prowl. Other beings quickly found doorways that slid to faraway places or hid in corners, moving through the gelatinous walls that were everywhere. Anything to get out of its path.

"I've been waiting for you," said Wolfstan, standing up straighter. It wasn't long before the sparks were running up and down his body as he gritted his teeth, the familiar dull pain settling in the middle of his chest. "Is this your way of checking me out or you just get off on torturing the living?" The rolling energy undulated, a ripple going down the middle. "Ah, so a little of both. I get it," he said, trying to catch his breath.

Not for the first time, Wolfstan wondered if he died

right there, would some form of him go on, trapped forever in a place that was neither here nor there?

He shook his head, focusing on the one thing that mattered most to him. *Revenge, always revenge.* He swallowed hard and pressed the hard end of the stump against his belly. "The groundwork has been laid. I've done what you asked and left signs everywhere out there in the world. The trap is set, even if some of them don't even know it yet. Soon enough, you'll have more powerful prey."

The Dark Mist slid around the entity, drawing closer even as the dead that were ensnared inside of the black tide reached out, grasping at nothing.

"Before I carry out part two, my needs will have to be met. A deal's a deal," he said, smiling with only a hint of nerves. "Leira Berens is mine to destroy. I want to see her face when she realizes everything she loves is being torn apart. Then you can have her."

The sparks intensified, flashes of light in what was usually a dimly lit place at best, jumping along his skin, leaving red welts down his neck and arms but Wolfstan held his ground.

"Pain only gets me excited." Wolfstan's voice came out in a higher pitch. "Lose me, lose your emissary to the land of the living. Who else would volunteer to deal with you?"

The energy drew back, the Dark Mist still swirling around at the bottom.

"Good," said Wolfstan. "We understand each other." Beads of sweat rolled down his pained face. "Then, next we take on the new Fixer. We missed Mara Berens and that can't happen again. This time, I'm in charge. Soon enough, I'll lay him at your feet."

The billowing dark energy pulled back, the sparks dissipating leaving Wolfstan lightheaded. "Well?" His head was swimming.

The Dark Mist slid away from the tear leaving it exposed. "That's a good start but you know what I need. Now or never, never at all."

The energy drew closer, the sparks jumping around everywhere, this time enveloping Wolfstan, seeping into his skin. "At last," he muttered, the taste of copper pennies in his mouth. Slowly, the whites of his eyes disappeared, and his eyes became black marbles. It wasn't long before he smiled broadly, crawling through the opening and into the world of the living, setting off to find his target.

# CHAPTER THIRTEEN

Matthew Moss folded his clothes neatly in a pile, putting the hiking boots to the side and shoving all of it under the rocky overhang. He stood up, naked and shivering, but not for long. The transformation into fur and fangs would make the icy air the perfect temperature.

He rubbed his arms, taking one last look around, still hidden by the dense woods in Shenandoah National Park. It was one of his favorite haunts to run with his pack. Plenty of trails that went on for miles with no tourists or hikers after dark who might get caught in the fray of large wolves running together under the light of the moon.

Even if someone managed to stay in the park, the hundred and five miles of mountainous terrain had plenty of hidden places where the shifters could take cover, and still keep moving.

"Here we go," he muttered, bracing himself. He felt the transformation starting to take over and grimaced, dropping back to his knees, banging them against the hard ground. It was always the same. He felt his bones crunch and glide, taking a new shape as his knees and elbows began to bend in the opposite direction. Stiff fur poked out of his skin in neat rows and his teeth grew longer and pointed.

Eventually, a large grey wolf stood amongst the pine trees, listening to the treetops creak in the wind. The wolf reared back his head and howled. A long cry that could be heard for miles. It didn't take long before there were other shifters responding to their leader with long, drawn out howls overlapping each other. The alpha could make out each individual and knew just how far away they were. He cried out again, baying loudly and calling the pack to assemble near him.

Shifter wolves moved in from different corners of the northern section of the park, being careful not to be seen, just in case.

A hiker would have mistaken the movement of the branches for the wind passing through the forest, but the large alpha wolf could hear the padded feet of twenty wolves gently hitting the ground and growing closer.

Large, furry heads with pointed ears finally poked through different sections of the underbrush, panting heavily. A few jostled for position, growling and snapping at each other. The grey wolf let out a short bark and bared his teeth, his breath turning into a warm vapor in the cool night air. No one tried to challenge him.

Once the pack was settled, the alpha slowly turned and stood on the edge of the rock face at Timber Hollow Overlook, looking out over the woods below.

The only movement was the occasional rabbit that dared to run quickly across the open ground, heading for home. Everything else was quiet. The wolf felt an urge to take off after the easy prey but resisted. Tonight was supposed to be an easy run, stretch the limbs and test the muscles. No blood sport this time out.

He moved out, staying low to the ground, still cautious and scanning the area. Reports of large wolves roaming the national park would only draw attention and mean the pack would have to avoid the area for at least a few months till the clamor died down. But after a mile, the muscular wolf felt himself starting to relax and picked up the pace. The wolves that were behind him, lined up according to rank within the pack, followed suit. It wasn't long before they were all running as fast as they could, jumping across short spans and winding down paths that led behind waterfalls or in between trees that towered above them, headed for the Dean Mountain Gap miles away.

It felt good to finally be running. It had been too long. All the troubles between the different magicals had come too close to the shifters, even if most magicals refused to acknowledge their existence most of the time. Small skirmishes between magicals were happening all over the D.C. area, crossing into the different parks, especially at night.

Most of their haunts had become too crowded and put them at risk of being exposed.

This was their last refuge, at least for now.

They were coming close to Rapidan Camp, crossing over a shallow section of South River. The ice cold water felt good across the grey wolf's broad chest, the fur wet with sweat. As they came up the far embankment that's when he smelled it, slowing down to take a good measure of the odor wafting up from a nearby shallow pool.

Something was wrong.

He barked three short yips, turning to face the approaching wolves, growling and baring his sharp teeth. The others immediately halted in their tracks, some backing up to a stand of trees that gave more cover. The alpha started to make his way down, taking his time. Another wolf, his closest ally, began to follow but the leader turned back and snapped at the air. The large, yellow wolf with white paws stared back at him, gently shaking his head.

They always faced danger together. The alpha took a moment but relented. After all, it was his own rule. No one goes toward danger alone, ever. The days of Lucius were behind them, and a new attitude prevailed among shifters everywhere. They worked together on everything. They had learned the hard way that community brought protection against the outside forces. And everyone else was considered an outside force.

Even Lucius had seen the light in the end.

The wolf grew closer, watching the steam rise out of the small, deep iridescent blue and black pool. His head grew lighter with each step closer. The foul smell filled his nostrils, making his dark black nose twitch. Something inside of it had been rotting for a while.

It wasn't long before his head was pounding and his thoughts became jumbled. He backed up instinctively, stumbling over the rocks and rough terrain. His hind legs bent, letting his tail graze along the ground.

The yellow wolf bound down toward him, biting him on the scruff of his neck and pulling him roughly toward higher ground. It wasn't easy to move the hundred- and thirty-pound wolf.

A front paw slid on the rocks sending a large, smooth pebble flying into the stench of the pool. It hit the surface, sending out ripples. But instead of slipping through the surface, the oily blue waters pulled back, revealing a dark inner chamber. The rock dropped with a distant thud as if it were dropped from a great height against solid ground. No splash at all.

The edges of the water drew back together, quickly appearing calm once again.

The other wolves responded in fear and anger, barking and howling at nothing in particular. All of them had been around long enough to see dangerous magical traps set just for them.

The grey wolf lay on his side, the rocks and twigs digging into his side. He waited till his breathing slowed down and the nausea settled. His friend never left his side, standing over him, but his head on a pivot looking for intruders who wanted to take advantage of the situation. Nothing stirred.

Finally, the prone wolf raised his head high enough to give it a good shake and rose slowly, his legs trembling, but holding his weight. He sneezed several times, shaking his body as his vision cleared and the pounding in his head stopped.

He took off at a slow run in the direction of his clothes, giving himself a chance to slowly recover. His lungs still felt tight, and he wasn't as sure of himself, avoiding the wider gaps and taking the longer route, passing from ridge points, down along the ground and back up again, over and over. Steadily, the pace quickened as he pressed the limits.

A wave of nausea washed over him, but he kept going, letting it pass and began to run. The yellow wolf was close to his right flank, still keeping watch of the surroundings even as they ran through the forest.

Not far behind was the rest of the pack, fanned out in an inverted V-shape, silently keeping pace, looking for trouble.

Once they were at their leader's pile of clothes everyone quietly waited. It wasn't long before the wolf lay down letting the transformation overtake him. Bones crunched and slid, hair receded, and teeth smoothed out till Matthew Moss lay along the cold ground, shivering once again.

He stood up, letting the wolves press in closer, their warm fur against his legs.

"A portal," he muttered, another shallower wave of nausea rolling across him. "But to where, and why?" He pointed to the north and nodded, sending the wolves toward their possessions. Time to head home to the safety of suburbia. His pants felt cold against his skin as he pulled them up. Something was nagging at him. "Was that a trap for us?"

"Seemed like more of an entrance to someplace I never want to go." A tall, lean man with light blonde hair emerged from the underbrush. "You need to tell your friends. That bounty hunter and the Fixer."

"Marcus. Thanks for saving my ass back there."

Marcus rubbed the close beard on his chin. "That was too close. Tell them, before someone is hurt."

"Yeah, if it hasn't happened already. Leira and Correk. I was having the same idea. That place, it smelled of death but not like a grave."

"Like death that was still moving around," said Marcus, finishing the thought.

## CHAPTER FOURTEEN

Yumfuck sat on an overturned metal pail, stretched to three feet tall to match the height of his new acquaintances, five Willens crowded around two old tires stacked one on top of the other with a bent piece of plywood on top.

The trolls who frequented the Taco Bell near the Potomac River had told him, these were the Willens he needed to befriend. The senior Willen was generally suspicious of everyone and reluctant to meet outsiders, much less help them. He never gave his name, preferring to remain anonymous. But if Yumfuck could persuade him, he held sway with hundreds of other networks of Willens everywhere. The large, old Willen was key to the plan he was forming. But first, the troll would need to earn his respect, even if there wasn't much time.

A large metal tray sat on the ground nearby, filled with day old bread, crusty cinnamon rolls and stale donuts. Yumfuck had already had three of the donuts, his sharp teeth easily biting through the tough exterior. Dried sugar clung to the fur around his mouth that he occasionally licked, his tongue swirling in a neat circle.

The troll held his cards close to his chest, smiling at the close cousins of New York City rats. Friendly enough, except when they felt cheated in some way. Their kind could dish it out but would only tolerate similar behavior in the closest of friends. Pulling it off with some finesse always helped as well.

Yumfuck glanced down at his cards, barely lifting them off his furry chest. A pair of fours, an ace and a queen. He was careful not to screw up his nose in frustration in front of the cluster of Willens surrounding their makeshift card table. Willens were known for their ability to quickly read any situation from the smallest of details. It's what made them so clever at permanently borrowing anything or cheating at cards.

Still, their honesty when asked a direct question was legendary in the magical realm of two worlds. The troll knew better than to ever turn his back on a Willen, but he knew he could trust their word.

It's why he was there. He was in need of information, but he knew better than to just ask for anything. There would need to be some give and take, a little bartering, and some decent smack talk first. Maybe a cinnamon roll. He reached out for one of the last two rolls, neatly stabbing it and shoving it whole into his mouth, his cheeks bulging, without ever taking his eyes off the game.

The largest of the Willens scratched his greying belly with sharp claws, moving aside his green velvet vest festooned with a mishmash of medals. One of them showed a young figure skater with her leg in the air, another had a military ribbon attached to a bronze circle representing the Light Elves of Oriceran. Another was a bronze star painted a pale blue in the center. Pinned just underneath it was a silver butter knife with a red ribbon around it. It seemed to oddly fit in with the entire display.

The troll was wearing his favorite navy blue felt vest with different mismatched silver pins attached and shiny brass buttons he polished just for this occasion. It never hurt to get the Willens' heart racing with a little envy. It made bartering later just a little easier.

He tapped the back of his cards, being careful not to smudge them with the bits of sparkly powdered sugar clinging to the fur on his chest. The stars and moons on the back of each card shifted with every tap. A common trait of Oriceran playing cards. The two moons were currently shining brightly on the back of his ace, casting a dim shadow onto the plywood tabletop. Yumfuck carefully unpinned a leaf made of silver from his chest, making a show of it, and pushed it toward the center of the table to sit among the other bauble and shiny coins.

"I call," he chirped, hesitating until one of the younger Willens laid out his cards. A collection of different cards with no kind of strategy. Yumfuck smiled, familiar with Willen strategy. They often played as a clan with outsiders, preferring to even lose a few hands, the younger ones making no attempt to win.

Yumfuck laid out his hand. Only a pair with an ace. Not much to speak of but respectful enough that it didn't look like he was throwing the game. A slap to every Willen that might lead to a brawl or at least the end of their afternoon together.

The other Willens snorted and jostled each other, whiskers on each of their faces twitching in delight. The troll sat back, doing his best not to look satisfied that his ruse was working.

The older Willen sat forward and tapped the plywood with a yellow claw. He laid out his cards, showing a run of eight, nine and ten. All with pulsing red hearts on them. The troll leaned forward, a look of surprise planted on his face. He shrugged and sat back. "This round is yours."

The elder Willen reached out his paws and drew the pot of shiny objects toward him, still eyeing the troll. "You are bonded with the Jasper Elf." He wasn't smiling or frowning, instead studying Yumfuck. "She has been a friend to our kind, more than once." The Willen tilted his head to one side, his round eyes narrowing. "What is it you need?" He waved a paw, the long, yellow claws slicing through the air. "Don't bother protesting. No troll anywhere ever played so miserably. Besides, amateurs don't show up with these kinds of cards." He tapped the cards, the planets reorganizing themselves every time. Oriceran, Mars, Earth, the star belt of Odin.

"Does the Elf know you're here?"

"Not in so many words."

The Willen laughed, his ample belly shaking the table. "We are not so different." He leaned even further into the tabletop, shoving the tires a few inches, his belly resting on the top of the plywood. "Life is more fun with a little game, a little risk and plenty of friends around you. Am I right?"

"Throw in a few snacks, maybe a donut or two and that's my life motto." Yumfuck cackled, brushing the fur on his chest, releasing a few sticky sprinkles from a forgotten donut a few days ago.

"You wear food like I wear medals."

"Proudly and a little bit of everything." The troll straightened his vest, letting some of the silver twinkle in the sunlight. Powdered sugar drifted down, some landing on the pins. Yumfuck licked a paw and wiped it off, licking his paw again. "Yummm, still good." He sat back, the muscles in his arms flexing just a little. The game was over and the food was almost gone. Soon, the Willens would just get up and go. Off to look for the next adventure. It was time for him to finally ask or let it go. There was no need for any further small talk.

"There's a new player in this world." Yumfuck leaned forward, the smile still on his face, even if his tone had changed. The pins on the vest rattled and banged against the board. "They're base of operations may be located in the Worst of All Possible Places."

The Willens shuddered as a group. The troll had used their nickname for the World in Between. Their fear of it was so great they had come up with a new name.

"Not possible." The elder Willen banged on the wooden board hard enough to make the cards slide from left to right. Yumfuck kept looking at the Willen, the smile fixed but he gathered up the cards, carefully making them into a neat pile. The planets and stars settling into one pattern. The deck would need to be returned to its rightful owner at some point.

"Now you see my problem, which could become our problem." The smile slipped from his face. "Whatever or whoever it is, keeps coming for my person. Leira Berens isn't safe. I'm not sure she even understands that yet." He looked over the heads of the Willens into the distance. "I have always been able to keep her safe. This time will not be any different." His voice cracked a little at the end and he cleared his throat. He carefully took off his vest, one of his favorites, and laid it in the center of the table. "I need your help. A tear in the Worst of All Possible Places has been spotted and there may be more openings. Will you alert your network and search for them."

The older Willen recoiled, his eyes growing wide and his whiskers trembling. A rare sight.

Yumfuck held up his paws. "I know what I'm asking and it's too much, except this time it's not. If someone or something has figured out a way to cross back and forth between this place -- and that -- then how long will it be before others slide into this world? And there's the bigger, badder, motherfucking question. What is so powerful that it can leave holes in place and stop anything else from using them?"

The Willen looked down at his worn leather sneakers, the laces in knots and a hole near the toe, letting a claw peek out. He looked up at Yumfuck, his forehead wrinkled with concern. "I will do my best to persuade my brethren. There is no worse fate for a Willen than to get sucked into that place. We are chased till we're caught, tortured and killed. There has been no other ending for my kind, and it has happened too many times." He let out a deep sigh as Yumfuck patiently waited. He knew the Willen understood what the future might hold if they did nothing, and it was worse. "But if you're right, we still have time on our side."

"It may be the only thing we have on our side," muttered Yumfuck, but the Willen still heard him.

"You've seen this monster?"

"I've seen its emissary and I've heard rumors from others." Yumfuck absently licked the sugar off his fur, calming himself. It was the secret he had not shared with Leira or Correk, yet. Not till he knew more. "A black tide filled with those who are neither dead or alive. Others have said they've seen it. This thing that has washed down their street, overtaking other magicals and sucking them into whatever the fuck it is."

The Willen shut one eye, and almost the other, staring at the troll. "You haven't told the one you're bonded with. Isn't that a violation of some unwritten rule? Why keep it to yourself?"

"Because she would run toward it, searching for answers before someone was hurt. This thing, though --" He hesitated, feeling the stale donuts turn over in his stomach. "It may be the evil we all didn't see coming that can't be stopped. At least, not without a lot of sacrifice." There it was. What the furry troll knew to be true. "The odds don't look like they're in our favor." A shudder passed through him that he did his best to hide.

The Willen stood on his back legs, the others joining him. "Then we are wasting time worrying ourselves. You came to the right place. Our kind knows how to hear things, see things without rushing too close to the danger." He fingered the vest, admiring the different silver pins with his other paw.

"Take it," said Yumfuck. "It's small payment. More of a tribute and a thank you for even trying." He rose off the bucket. "Stay safe," he said solemnly. "May we all meet up again and play another round of cards on the other side of all this."

The Willen grasped the vest tightly to his chest. He put out his paw. "Reginald. My name is Reginald."

The gesture was an act of kinship reserved for a very few. He shook the Willen's paw. "I am Yumfuck Tiberius Troll. It's an honor to be working with you."

Reginald laughed, despite the situation. "If I'd known it was you, I would have brought more food. I've heard stories about you. They can't all be true."

"True and then some." The troll leaned back and let out a loud *whoop, whoop* that rose up from his belly.

Already, some of the Willen were leaving, making their way toward the nearest storm drain and lifting the grate, slipping inside and disappearing from sight.

"You can leave me word at --"

Reginald was down on all four legs, his new treasures already hidden in the folds of his skin. "We will find you," he said, cutting off Yumfuck. "There are always Willens who know where everyone is to be found. We will not fail you. And we will have that card game. Maybe the next time you will give it more of an effort." He turned and jogged to the open grate, neatly sliding in despite his girth.

Yumfuck watched him go and then shrunk down to his miniature size, gathering up the cards to put in his rucksack. "I hope you're right, Reginald," he squeaked. He let out a sigh. "I'm not sure anyone understands what is coming for us, but they will."

Mara searched her desk drawer, carefully taking out everything inside of it, searching for her favorite deck of cards. "They have to be here. I know I put them in here, wrapped in that silk handkerchief."

"You say something?" Professor Lucy Fowler poked her head into the office, her wild, frizzy red hair surrounding her face. "We've just about gotten the smell out of the great hall."

"What? Good work, I knew you could do it. No," she said, waving her hand. "Just looking for something." She pulled out a few old pens and felt something sticky clinging to her fingers. A green, stained post-it note slid out and she flipped it over. "Borrowed your cards. Will take good care of them," she read out loud. The note was signed with a tiny paw print. "Yumfuck!" she yelled into the empty space of the room. "What are you up to? Those were my good cards!"

## CHAPTER FIFTEEN

Night was falling quickly in Austin, the sky holding onto the last of the red and purple streaks that went on forever. No one in the crowded parking lot of the Carousel Lounge noticed. They were too focused on the battle that was threatening to break out.

Magicals of every ilk were broken into two clear groups, facing off with each other.

"Now wait a minute! Wait one long minute!" Uncle Petie stood between the two groups; his long, thin arms outstretched. Small, bright flames danced on the ends of each of his fingers. He was dressed in silver, billowy pants decorated with moons and stars and there was a top hat, bent ever so slightly on the rim, balancing on the side of his head. A mouse peeked out from under the hat and saw the crowds, ducking back under but not before pulling the hat to a less precarious position.

A Gnome in leather overalls with faded knee patches raised a flame thrower enhanced with magic and clicked off the safety. Uncle Petie saw the gesture and without moving his head, sent the flames in the Gnome's direction, cutting a straight and fiery line that warmed the Gnome's boots, melting just the tip of the soles. "Next time it'll be a closer line," growled Uncle Petie. He was done playing the nice host. "Keep it up and someone is getting barbecued tonight, Texas style. You'll be the special next week."

The Gnome hesitated but reset the safety, even if he didn't lower his weapon. He was standing among a horde of thugs, felons and malefactors looking to hunt Silver Griffins for the pleasure and the profit and a little revenge.

On the other side were Witches and Wizards, former Silver Griffin agents who had been hiding out at the Carousel Lounge, waiting to move on to new identities. All of them stood ready, their wands raised. Behind them, hidden by Uncle Petie's staff, were their children huddled in a quivering crowd.

Someone had ratted them out. That was what was really making Uncle Petie's acid reflux boil, and no one wanted to see what that might cause. Uncle Petie had been a good and loyal friend to both sides of this argument over the years. He was a refuge of last resort for all kinds, and everyone knew it. His magical seal, a silver foil elephant wearing a top hat, hidden in any document, could open doors for the desperate in all kinds of dark places, on two different worlds.

But for the very unlucky few who got on his permanent bad side, there was no place they could go and hide anymore. Every other hidey hole would honor Uncle Petie's decision and turn them away too. A target would forever be on their back, until they met with an untimely and most likely torturous death, and both sides knew that too.

"Anyone else want to try my patience?" Uncle Petie spat out the words, his entire body trembling, making the silver pants shimmer in the parking lot lights. No one else moved. "This is fucking neutral ground! Always has been and will remain so long past when all of you are ashes, however long that doesn't take." He turned his attention toward the motley crew of dark magicals standing uphill and the furthest away from the Carousel Lounge. "Go now, or I'll consider this your acknowledgment that you and I are done trading, permanently. Leave the vicinity and all of Austin for thirty days. Your punishment for even attempting a coup on my property. Violate my edict by even an inch and I'll put the word out on you to everyone I know, and to every corner."

A dark Wizard stirred, grunting and tapping his wand against his leg.

"Try me, Lincoln. You can go first, if you like. I suspect the Richley Brothers will finally have their revenge on you, within the week. Plenty of those standing near you will turn you in. I hear there was a premium on that bounty."

The magicals standing closest to the Wizard took a few steps back, eyeing him differently. Some of them sizing him up and checking their magical bandwidths for any reports of a bounty on him. Lincoln curled his lip but vanished in a puff of smoke. A cheap trick but effective.

"What about you, Delancey? Or Rider? Millview?" Uncle Petie kept naming each of them, one at a time. A thinly veiled threat. He was famous for knowing everyone. He gave no other details, not stating outright who was wanted or not, but it was a good guess that most of them had crossed the wrong magical at one point in their dark careers.

One by one, they began opening portals or stomping off into the darkness, or pulling the same trick as Lincoln for a little added drama and a puff of smoke. It wasn't long before there were only a few left and once they took a look around at the number of skilled former agents, and Uncle Petie, facing them, even they gave up with a sigh and left.

Finally, at least half of the parking lot was empty. The mouse peeked out from Uncle Petie's hat again and squeaked, curling back up under the hat, letting it fall back into place. Uncle Petie pulled out a handkerchief that never ended, draping down his side, and patted the sweat off his forehead. "Never should have gotten this far," he snarled. There was a bitter taste in his mouth. "No respect for the rules. Someone will have to be an example. Lincoln will do," he muttered.

He lowered his hands, the flames going out, tiny tendrils of smoke wafting up from his fingertips. He snapped his fingers, eliciting sparks that formed themselves into the outline of an envelope with the name, *Richley* hanging in gold sparks in the center, and sped away. Lincoln's fate was sealed.

It was necessary if Uncle Petie were to maintain his unique form of neutrality. Everyone had to know there were harsh consequences for their actions. No exceptions.

A pale, middle aged witch with long, stringy blonde hair and dark circles under her eyes stepped closer to Uncle Petie. "Is that it? Can we go back inside?" Her eyelids drooped for a moment like she hadn't slept in days, which was probably true. Too many of the agents were using spells or potions to stay alert at all times, but eventually something had to give.

Uncle Petie's face softened, and he absently curled the end of one side of his moustache back into a proper curl, even though it wasn't necessary. "Yes, the coast is clear. No one will be foolish to come back tonight. Go find a bed and rest your eyes. You'll need it. We are not done with this nonsense, not yet." He raised his hands over his head and gave a short clap. "Everyone, go back inside and get something to eat or find the nearest cot and take care of yourselves. You're safe here. I've seen to that, again."

The collective of Witches and Wizards reluctantly turned and found their spouse, or children and shuffled back inside the doors painted on the outside to look like a circus tent folded back. Uncle Petie took one last long look back at the dimly lit parking lot, an uneasy feeling coming over him, before following them inside. He paused, listening to the lock magically catch and turn in several directions until he was satisfied enough to go take up his usual spot behind the bar.

---

Outside, in the shadows of the far reaches of the large parking lot, a Wizard and Witch emerged under the farthest streetlamp, sniffing the air. "Smells rancid. Just the way I like it," said the Witch, wrinkling her nose. The pair were seeking out the different trails of dark magic that were still lingering behind the magicals who had reluctantly departed. The Wizard held up his wand, twirling it in a lazy circle as the dark trails wove themselves together, disappearing into the palm of his hand. Just beneath his palm, peeking out from his neat, white shirt was a violet-colored R intertwined with a P.

"Did we get enough to trace them?" asked the Witch, keeping watch to make sure no one saw them.

"More than enough." He licked his palm, savoring the acrid burn on the tip of his tongue that came from so much energy being stirred together. "Let the games begin." The corners of his mouth curled up ever so slightly as he opened a portal. "After you," he said with a slight bow. "First up, Millview. He was there in Chicago when the vault collapsed. This should be satisfying."

"Let's make his ending last," said the Witch, stepping through the portal. "I have nowhere else to be tonight."

"As you wish," said the Wizard, stepping carefully behind her, letting the portal close with a quiet hiss.

## CHAPTER SIXTEEN

Leira stood in the center of the forest, long, dry, brown pine needles crunching under her boots.

Tess sat perched on the edge of an old, rotting stump, her milky eyes searching back and forth for signs only she could see, and not much else. Her long white, wavy hair was tied back loosely with the stem from a dandelion. Still, wisps escaped and floated on the breeze near her face. "Listen to the conversations that are all around you," said the ancient seer. "What do you hear?"

It was their third lesson in as many days. Her newly found skills were growing but the execution was still spotty. *Let go and work with, all at once. Tap my head and rub my belly, basically.*

Leira took a deep breath and let it out slowly, listening to the sound of her breath leaving her lungs. Two birds chattered overhead, vying for attention. The wind let out a low whistle moving through the tree branches.

Nearby, she could hear the troll digging under some leaves, looking for grub worms to race. She had already warned Yumfuck not to take any of them home to use in his tiny race cars. She still wasn't sure he was listening.

Tess gently clapped her hands together and smiled. "Pay attention, dear. Yumfuck can take care of himself."

Leira studied Tess's face once again, wondering how she knew.

"I can see what really matters." Tess's smile widened, creating deep lines in her face. "Now, create a space for yourself and be still. You are capable of doing the same. Let everything else go. Listen to what is usually missed by the preoccupied, which is almost everything that walks on two legs." She raised her hands near her head as if she was using them to tune into something.

Leira felt the energy stirring at her feet. It was bubbling up into her ankles just underneath her skin. She saw the backside of the troll poke out and shake to its own beat before sliding under a pile of leaves. He was dragging a plastic baggie behind him.

"Let it all go," she muttered, as the world around her began to fade and blend together in a watercolor smear, shutting her eyes. The troll's chirping reached her ears, and she felt an urge to open her eyes, take a look, but a second thought came over her, the energy pulling her along. *Listen to the sounds no one else hears.*

She opened her eyes again and all the colors around her had sharpened and become more distinctive. Her breath was now the background to different layers of sound that kept going deeper. The usual sounds were a distraction and she knew it. There was a different choice to be made, to listen to something else.

The energy was coursing through her at a steady, pulsing rate she had never experienced before.

Once or twice she tried to zero in on the flow, only to feel overwhelmed. It was like trying to hug a raging river.

Tess's voice was a whisper in her head. "Let go and let the river carry you."

Leira's lips moved but no sound came out. *Let the river carry me.*

"Oof!" Her breath rushed out in a gasp. "What the fuck is happening?"

"So many things. Surrender to it."

Leira heard the deeper layers of nature all talking at once. It wasn't a voice or words, exactly. It was a sense of knowing that came over her; of what should come next, what plant or animal was asking for help, and directions about where things needed to be.

Everything in nature suddenly presented itself to her as an interlocking puzzle of a million moving pieces doing an elegant dance.

"Nothing is ever out of place," she whispered, her mouth slowly opening in awe.

"Yes, my dear," said a satisfied Tess, a halo of light surrounding her head and small moths circling back and forth. "That is the real mystery and magic of this world. Most never see it."

Leira's eyes took on a glow but the symbols along her arms were quiet. All was well, and there was nothing to report. She turned in a slow circle, marveling at everything she could feel coming at her from every corner. As long as she was willing to be a part of it, control nothing, she could hear it all.

"I get it. I don't hear a thing with my ears."

"Quite right. It's with the deepest parts of yourself that you feel it, and some would call that listening. I do, in fact. Listening is not always about hearing. More often, it is all about feeling and connection. That requires a willingness to see oneself as a part of something and not separate, standing off to the side." The old seer rocked back and forth, humming an ancient tune.

Leira felt the nearby oak trees sharing moisture and nutrients, passing along what they could through their roots to trees further down the line that were in need and asking for help.

"Use all your senses. Breathe in deeply. What else is there for you? You are only at the beginning. Don't let your astonishment stop you from seeking more."

The trees right in front of her blended into the background and superimposed on top were rapidly moving clouds and rain falling gently hundreds of miles away. "What? The trees are sharing information on their surroundings. No--"

"Why no?" Tess's voice cut through everything else. "The trees are the steadfast guardians of our worlds. They see everything and are responsible for holding a lot of the balance. Surely, you have met a dryad or two in your travels."

The energy suddenly gripped Leira around the waist, pulling tight. Breathing became difficult. Images of Perrom's mother swam in her head, quickly followed by Ossonia. *I've let you down.* Leira felt herself wanting to grasp at solutions, taking back a feeling of control. The sounds and images began to dissipate.

Tess clicked her tongue. "You are never really in charge, Leira Berens. Have you not learned that yet? It's only ego and fear that tells us we need to be, and then we miss the most powerful magic of all."

Leira could only take sips of breath while trying to steady herself. The troll popped out of the leaves, his eyes wide, staring up at Leira. There was a pale blue line around the outline of his mouth.

"Stop telling yourself the old story, Leira. You are not the salvation of this world. You are a part of the answer. Granted, a very necessary part but once you can let go of such a heavy responsibility and become a mere part of what makes things work, then you will truly realize your power as a Jasper Elf with a touch of humanity. You will become unstoppable." Tess sharply clapped her hands three times and Leira felt the tension ease around her waist, even if the old scar had begun to burn.

"Ah, good," said Tess, "you still trust me. Your willingness is intact. Then all things are possible. Let go of this idea about what you must fix, or what you must do. Instead, humble yourself and ask for help, with no expectation of when the answer will appear. Or what it will be. Then you will see what magic can truly do."

Leira shut her eyes, trying to let go of the image of Ossonia falling into the World In Between. "I'm not sure how to do that."

"I know, and the first step is knowing that's okay. You don't need the answers."

Leria opened her eyes to see Tess swirl her hand overhead. She felt a womp of energy surge through her.

"Let go, Leira," said Tess, still circling her delicate

fingers in the air. "Try falling backward into the energy. See what happens. No, no. Keep your eyes open."

Yumfuck started to position himself in a place where he could catch her but a stern look from Tess stopped him.

Leira felt a shudder pass through her and looked up at the sky, patches of blue barely visible through the trees, as she let her body fall back, her arms still by her side. She felt herself going backward, branches passing her, but she did nothing to stop any of it. *All is well. Let the river carry me.* A calm came over her, even as the ground rapidly approached.

Just as suddenly, a billow of energy passed underneath her, and she found herself standing on her feet. Not quite sure how she got there.

Leira looked at her surroundings, a little unsure of everything she was seeing.

Tess pulled herself to her feet, leaning on an old, knotted stick that was equal to her height. "That's enough for now. You've had a taste and the seed has been planted. Stay open to what the world has to offer you, Leira Berens. We will practice again. Remember this," said Tess, leaning on the homemade cane. "Nature is always on your side, if you let it, and can be a powerful ally, but not by force. Not on your terms."

Leira bent down to scoop up the troll and turned around to say something to Tess, but the seer was gone without a sound. The different layers of the forest had retreated and all that was left behind were the sounds of the wind and the occasional bird or rabbit or deer moving through the woods.

Leira tucked the troll into her pocket, taking a long

look around before she turned back to the more practical. "Hand over the baggy, Yumfuck. I know you have it. Leave the critters out in the wild, please."

The troll reluctantly dragged the clear baggy out of the pocket, teeming with squirming white grubs. Leira held it up by a corner and crouched, opening the baggy and gently shaking out the contents. "Maybe it's time for another troll visit, Yumfuck. You need more friends."

"Maybe," said the troll, letting out a wistful sigh. He propped himself up on his elbows, just his head poking out of the pocket. "I felt the size of the wave of magic that passed through you," squeaked the troll. "Never have I ever," he said. "But for the first time in a while, I feel better about our chances."

Leira startled and her brow furrowed. "Chances about what?"

"You can feel it too. Something dark is approaching."

Leira looked back at the trees, trying to surrender again and felt the edge of the mysterious new magic. "Yeah, something is wrong. But what, exactly?"

"Time will tell us everything. Till then, I live to eat, play, love everything."

Leira scooped her hand into her pocket to feel the warm, soft fur and rub her thumb along his head. "Its own kind of surrender. I get it, or at least I'm starting to."

## CHAPTER SEVENTEEN

"Why are there three ketchup bottles? And what's with the five bags of coconut?" Correk stood in the narrow pantry of the brownstone shaking his head. He poked the bags of coconut as if that would yield him an answer and shook one of the bottles of ketchup. Yumfuck sat on his shoulder, patiently watching Correk take inventory.

"This is somehow your doing, isn't it?" asked Correk

The troll stood up and let out a laugh, leaping to the nearest shelf. "Not this time. Leira is distracted with other things, even more than usual." Yumfuck made his way to the back of the shelf and triumphantly lifted a can of tuna over his head. "There's six of these suckers back here but we're out of mayo and bread. Not sure what's up with the coconut."

"Nothing goes together. And why is there so much rice?"

The troll disappeared, tunneling under a loosely assembled pile of different pasta, only to emerge with a bag of dry split-peas. "You could go to the store. That's occurred to you, right?"

"The last time I came home with that lettuce spinner. I'm not sure there's room in this kitchen for me to go to the store. The gadgets they have in this world. Where is that thing, anyway?"

The troll had already moved on, pushing his way behind an oversized jar of chunky peanut butter. He hugged it warmly. "I will see you again, later. No need to mention to anyone the hole down the center of the jar," he whispered.

"I can hear you and I already know," said Correk, arching a brow. "And I've seen all the bits of fur blended into the rest. That's one way to make sure you get all of it."

"Occupational hazard." Yumfuck clapped his little paws together. "Pay attention, Fixer."

Correk stopped searching the shelves for anything to sample. He took a step back, his brow furrowed and his hands on his hips, staring at the troll.

"That's better. Leira is distracted," said the troll, pointing a tiny claw at Correk. "You are her mate. You're missing the signs. That's not good for anyone." He threw his tiny paws in the air. "Yes, she's always got half her attention focused on some danger, and there's always danger. This is different. Something larger, darker and more powerful is out there and Leira can sense it. I can feel it," he said, patting his chest. "Her magic, those symbols on her arms, they're all future predictors. It's like some part of her is always calculating risk and this time it's come up in a very bad, not good, going to go horribly way."

Correk slowly rubbed his chin, his fingers rubbing

against rough day-old bristles. "I did know," he said, slowly. "But there is no sign, no real sign of anything worse, yet. Nothing worse than what's happened in the last year." He bent low, his face inches from the Yumfuck's. "What else do you know?"

Yumfuck wrinkled his nose and waved a paw in front of his face. "You mean, besides your inexplicable love of onions and garlic in your eggs? Okay, okay, fine but we've talked about this," he squeaked, pressing his paws to his round belly.

"You're delaying. It's that bad?" Correk pinched the bridge of his nose, sweeping his long, blonde braid off his shoulder. "Yumfuck, on my word as an Oriceran, tell me what you know or..."

"You're a busy elf. Nothing except the rumors." The troll pressed his eyes shut, swallowing hard. He opened them again, worry in them. Something a troll rarely showed. "There are advantages to my sizes, big and small. This one," he said, opening his arms wide, "is that I hang out with all the smallest creatures that none of you bipedal giants ever even notices. All the tiny and smaller model size magicals that are everywhere."

"Get to the point." Correk lifted his head, listening. A magical was in trouble. He tilted his head to the right, surprised. The cacophony was deafening.

"I get it. Work call and you have to take it. No worries, go, go."

But without the troll's usual bravado the sense of some unknown danger getting too close only grew inside Correk. He stood very still, waiting on Yumfuck.

The troll gave up and his shoulders sagged. "Speaking any of this out loud makes it worse. You know that."

"It makes it possible to come up with a plan, an antidote."

"If there is one."

"There is always one. I still believe that." There it was again. *What kind of danger is causing that?* Correk's ears twitched. "Tell me, *now*."

"I suppose this was inevitable and the day is finally here. Fine, fine, I'll speed it up. All of these critters trade info, barter with it. It's their main stock in trade, so all of them pay attention to everything. They're all lit up lately over information that keeps getting picked up by different organisms all over the world." The troll leaned in and whispered the news he had tucked away, waiting for the right moment, or more news, or even better, to find out it was false. "The World in Between, that blob that chases Leira. It's become sentient and has been gathering souls, or energy, or magic. The glo-worms, yes, they have feelings, they've seen it happen. That dark tide has reached for magicals just as a tear opens in a portal. *Slurp!* Gone, obliterated. No more. Whatever you want to call it. It has a cast of thousands trapped in there and it only wants more."

Correk straightened up, slowly taking a breath and looking around the pantry as if something in there would help him with an answer. "Jasper energy. The unending light."

"With every magical it gathers, it gains a nuance to its magic, gleaned from the poor slob it's absorbing. Yeah, yeah, anyone not skilled enough to open a decent portal and fall into that realm doesn't have much to offer the

Dark Mist. But multiply that by thousands, and then thousands more and give it years to build and suddenly." The troll stopped and held out his paws with a shrug. He let the silence hang between them for a moment. "Something else. There is suddenly a very different component, though. Like that creepmeister got itself a supercharge."

"Wolfstan Humphrey." A chill crept down Correk's spine. He turned his head again. The call was growing even more urgent. "I have to go." He picked up the troll and held him near his face. "But no more holding back information. Not a word, not a thought, not a suspicion, not a smell. Nothing."

"You mean from you," said Yumfuck, giving Correk's nose a boop. "Don't bother Leira, right? Correk, don't dig a hole and then pour the dirt on top of yourself by admitting it. Let's leave it at, you said nothing." The troll bit his bottom lip. "Fuck me. Fine, you will know what I know, not too long after I know it. I will need a little time for contemplation and integration." The troll shook his head, his tiny paws crossed behind his back. "Don't argue, you don't have time right now. Go and be the background hero. There's nothing to do yet, anyway. Trouble will still be hunting us in a few hours."

Correk set the troll back down on the shelf, his jaw set. He quietly slung the spare bow and quiver over his shoulder that he kept in the corner of the pantry and opened a portal, careful to check the edges, just in case. A small sign that the edges of the danger were getting to him. Very unlike a Fixer.

There was nothing more to say. There were no words to add to what Yumfuck had said. The Dark Mist was becoming sentient, or already was, and in his elven bones he knew, Wolfstan had something to do with all of it.

Finally, there was a monster that might be able to take them all down. *Perhaps the old Fixer's library will have something.*

He stepped through the portal without looking back, greeted by the screeches, hoots, and yells of twenty different animals. Even the chaos of the scene in front of him of large, magical beasts running loose could not shake him out of the puzzle that he was trying to fix. It didn't matter that there weren't enough pieces yet to do anything but wonder. *How bad will this get?*

"Okay, be like that. Leave without a word. A little hurtful." Yumfuck waved a paw, even while he was slicing open one of the coconut bags, sampling the sweet shavings. He squished a handful of the shredded coconut between his paws, pushing the sticky mound into his mouth, puffing out the right cheek. "Enjoy the foibles of everyday magicals while you can, Fixer. These will soon seem like the best days." He slowly chewed the coconut, sitting down on the shelf. "Perhaps it's finally time to call in the cousins."

---

Correk stepped through the portal, only to lean back just as it closed to avoid an elephant stampeding in his path. The elephant had his trunk high overhead, trumpeting out a loud warning. Magical notes poured out playing a song normally reserved for marching into battle.

Three gray spider monkeys rode on his back, bouncing from one end to the other, screeching and waving their arms. They were frantically throwing pebble-sized fireballs back at whatever was following them on their path.

Gazelles that could leap over small homes and camels that were able to outrun horses and even lions with the familiar long, twisted horns were all snarling and snapping, growling and stomping to get themselves further away from whatever was chasing them.

Correk didn't hesitate and headed directly for the source. "The only way to change your path is to face the danger that's on it with you," he whispered, ignoring the pulse of energy racing across the back of his neck. It crackled and hissed making the fine hairs stand up on end.

He passed the concession stand painted cotton-candy-pink with green trim that sold soft pretzels and dancing monkey marionettes. On past the entrance to the monkey house with the large sign prohibiting the use of flashes or strong lights accompanied by an even longer message about the dire consequences.

Finally, taking the curve around the outdoor pen for the seals from the oceans of Oriceran who could walk upright on their large tail and had a language all their own made up of barks and squeaks.

But each place he passed, there were no animals to be seen or heard. All of the movement and noise was coming from behind him where he had just left. This part of the zoo was deserted. "Not a good sign."

*Clang!* A loud, metallic noise rung out from around the curve that would take someone up to the popular bird houses. *Clang, clang!*

The sound was growing louder as Correk cocked an arrow and picked up the pace, trotting toward the sound.

Coming down the hill was the zoo owner, an older Wizard, dressed in a loud, blue suit that was at least two sizes too large and billowed out around him. His wavy brown hair was caught in a thin ponytail.

Different bits and pieces of the zoo were clinging to him everywhere. Locks, part of a fence, a dog collar, a metal tray, a long piece of thick metal chain.

Correk heard a whizzing fast approaching and ducked in time to see a metal pole with a loop on one end fly over his head. It was coming straight at the owner and didn't stop, slamming sideways into his body and temporarily knocking the wind out of him. It wasn't long before there was a tinkling sound and all the coins from the concession stand were flowing along at a quick pace as if they were being carried by a breeze. They circled the zoo owner's body, making contact as if they were now his belt.

"Help me!" pleaded the man. "Something has gone wrong. All the animals are loose and the locks have failed. We need to do something before one side realizes there's an all-you-can-eat buffet running next to them, and the other side starts using magic to even the odds." *Bang!* A paperweight of a gleaming arch that read, St Louis hit him in the square of the back almost bringing him to his knees.

The man stretched out his arms toward the Fixer. Correk felt his knife that he always kept in his boot struggling to rip itself free and fly toward the owner. Correk whispered an ancient spell creating a protective barrier around himself and felt the knife relax. Step one.

"I didn't know, I didn't know," the owner wailed. It was an excuse Correk heard at least once a day as the Fixer.

The Wizard continued to stumble forward determined to get somewhere.

"Prohibere." A simple spell Correk sung out in the old Oriceran style. But as soon as he did, he saw the reason the wizard had persevered despite the growing weight, despite the locks being ripped off of cages setting even more animals and birds free.

The buildings right around them began to tremble as if the nails and beams that held them together were straining to be set free and engulf the zoo owner. Some kind of spell was still emanating from the Wizard to anything within a short radius.

Correk acted quickly, rolling a string of light down his arm that ran around the circumference of the Wizard, creating a circle six feet in diameter. The light lay on the ground, projecting upward into the air ghostly, pale grey images of twirling tornadoes holding onto whatever had the misfortune to be in their path.

The shaking began to slow and the buildings settled back onto their foundations. Even some of the animals seemed to sense that a certain kind of order was being restored and slowed their exits, even if they were still jogging toward a different destination.

However, a few suddenly realized they were still in peril from some of the other animals and wide-eyed took up running again. Correk opened his hand, revealing another small, slowly revolving twister and whistled a tune into it before setting it free to expand.

The magical twister blew out of his hand, falling apart and releasing a wind that swept across the zoo grounds, whipping up the grass and forgotten candy wrappers along the ground. The tune whistled inside the wind on a loop as it came across the animals, enveloping them, rustling their fur and swishing their tails. At first, it stopped all of them from running or eyeing each other like a snack or a predator. The elephant still struggled, despite the strong spell, raising its trunk to trumpet and protest but the wind prevailed, soothing the elephant, wrapping itself around the animal's wide girth and gently caressing the rough skin, blowing into the large ears, whispering comforting noises.

At last, the elephant relented and began to slowly move back toward its enclosure at the far end of the zoo at a much slower pace than the panicked exit. The monkeys sat quietly on her back, numb from all the commotion.

The Wizard tried to raise his arms in relief at the sight but the metal still clinging to him wouldn't let him. Instead, he finally fell to his knees under the weight, watching the elephant pass. "Belinda! Good girl, keep going. Tell the others," he cried out.

Belinda swung her trunk left and right, her large ears pressed flat against her head. She lumbered forward, exhausted from the remnants of fear and the hurried rush toward safety. But at last, she raised her trunk and sung out, the notes carrying over the other animals, blending harmoniously with the tune Correk had already sent.

At first it was just the lions, lightly bouncing on their paws as they made their way back to the lions' den, a large structure made of old stone. The hyenas were not far behind, already back to chatting noisily with each other. The birds came next. Pink flamingos and toucans flying just overhead made a steady stream of electric colors. A fluid wave of feathers and beaks that made an easy turn to the right to head up the path toward their airy cages that took up a city block.

The gazelles and antelopes trotted behind them keeping a respectful margin of space and it wasn't long before every creature in the zoo was back and resting comfortably in their home, despite the absence of locks. Nothing was trying to suddenly break free anymore.

Correk could finally turn his attention to the belabored zoo owner. He came and stood over him, working one spell and then another to lift off the weight but nothing was working, yet. Correk sensed the magical's exhaustion and finally was able to help by taking on some of the weight with a little used spell he had found in the back of a very small tome with a very thin spine.

"Turner Underwood was right, again. All spells eventually become useful. But if they're never known, none of them will work." He leaned closer to the Wizard, his muscular frame holding up most of the weight. "Ingram Wending, tell me the truth and do it quickly. Where did you get the spell and what were the words, exactly."

Ingram hesitated, relieved now that the animals were safe, and the weight was lessened. Correk rolled the fingers on one hand and the weight descended again. "Tell me and I can help you. Say nothing and I'll understand you don't want my help, and I'll leave. Decide quickly. I have other places to be."

*Wolfstan Humphrey.* The words rang in the Fixer's head.

"Okay, okay." Ingram pressed his hands against his head. "It was in an old book my cousin bought at the Dark Market. An old chapbook. Someone's private diary. Not a very long story." Ingram wearily shook his head. "I knew better, I swear I did, but it seemed harmless."

"You're not saying anything, yet." Correk arched a brow, tempted to at least start to open a portal.

Ingram's shoulders sagged. "Attendance has been down. This was supposed to be a spell of attraction. Bring in the crowds and help me save this place." He bowed his head.

"Say the first three words of the spell." Correk felt a familiar warm energy flowing through him. The Fixer's Elven magic mixing with the energy he acquired since taking over the post.

"Absalom, Absalom, rectify." He stopped abruptly, too afraid to keep saying the words.

Correk felt his own energy warm his chest in response to the dark spell. Ingram Wending had unwittingly called to the dark side, asking for a favor. Dark magicals had picked up the request and someone out there picked up the request.

Of course, Correk's counter spells weren't working because a barter was in play. "The animals," muttered Correk. "That was the payment."

"What? How can that be?"

"Easily," said Correk, taking up his bow again, getting ready. "You agreed to their terms when you said the spell. They set the ground rules. It's how it works in dark magic."

"Dark magic," sputtered Ingram, pulling some of the metal objects closer as if they could protect him.

It wasn't long before the emissaries arrived. Two large auburn hounds baring their fangs. They would want their payment or take Ingram instead. But Correk was ready, with no time to spare.

He created a vortex, tapping the edge of his bow hard on the ground, pulling back in just enough time to reverse the spell, voiding the agreement. One of Turner's favorite ploys.

The dogs snarled and snapped at the air but retreated all the same, stepping back into a portal. On the other side was an overgrown forest steeped in a thick fog and teeming with noise. Correk took a step forward, startled to see the imitation Dark Forest, minus the Gardener. "A new player?"

But the portal closed before he could get a longer look and just as quickly, the metal flew back to its original locations, completing the reversal. Correk held up a hand, snapping his fingers and felt the chapbook appear, nestled safely in his care. Another one to study and then file away somewhere where no one will find it.

Ingram lay flat on the ground, breathing hard. He opened his mouth as if he wanted to say something and then thought better of it. Correk held out a hand, helping the Wizard to his feet and steadying him. "You have a magical wonderland here. Humans will flock here just to see the Oriceran animals. Have them come by appointment. Make it an occasion. But cast no more spells aimed at them or when I come back, we will return these animals to their rightful world."

"Understood." Ingram was still shaking and his brow was damp with sweat, even with the dry wind still blowing around them. "You're not like the old Fixer. I met him a couple of times too," said Ingram with a shrug. "I suppose I'm a frequent flier. No punch card though. You could put that in your suggestion box." He tried a weak smile.

Correk was already opening a portal and stepping through. He was not as garrulous as Turner Underwood, and besides, there were more pressing things on his mind.

---

On the other side of the portal, Leira sat at the kitchen table holding a bagel out of reach of the troll who was dancing around anxiously on the table. "Ignore him," she said. "He got the entire other half. How was your day?"

"Interesting," said Correk, trying to memorize everything about his mate. Every curve, every line, every familiar movement. She gave him a crooked smile and tilted her head. He smiled back to reassure her, resting his bow on the tile floor and examining the scratches where he had tapped the hard ground. "A sturdy walking stick may be in my future," he said, trying to distract himself. *I will do anything to protect you.* It was the only thought in his head.

Yumfuck looked up at him, momentarily standing still. The fur along his back stood on end but he quickly brushed it down before Leira could notice. He went back to his pleading and Correk went to store his bow and quiver, kissing Leira on the top of the head as he passed. A spark passed from his lips, sliding under her skin sending a warm wave down to her toes. She laughed and looked up at him. "Maybe later," she said, smiling.

He smiled, ducking into the pantry, sucking in air between his teeth to stop himself from shouting. *Something is wrong and it's getting closer.*

## CHAPTER EIGHTEEN

Perrom moved easily through the denser parts of the Dark Forest where no one ever visited. No one ever dared to venture into those parts. These were the most remote sections stretching on for miles in every direction, full of clever and unseen traps set by the Gardener, and legend said there was even a garden of statuary in the darkest parts. Foolish trappers who had ventured into the forest and were dealt with by the Gardener.

No one knew for sure if it was legend or fact, and no one was willing to go on an adventure to prove it. The Gardener was mostly mythical as well outside the forest and his storied devotion to the flora and fauna were whispered about in pubs nearest the edges of the sanctuary. It was home to many species long forgotten outside the forest. Everyone knew that magicals rated fairly low on the Gardener's scale. Best to avoid the Dark Forest altogether whenever possible,

But the Wood Elf had grown up in the forest, investigating every part of it as a boy and knew all of his father's tricks. Or at least had convinced himself he did. His mother, the Dryad had even taught him how to use the trees as allies. After all, he was half-Dryad and could disappear into the trees when necessary.

He was panting, his chest rising and falling more from expectation than exertion. "Slow down, listen." His mother's constant advice that was always buzzing in his head, whether he liked it or not. These days, there wasn't a lot he could find to like.

Unless it had something to do with his one quest. To free Ossonia from the World in Between. "My fault, my fault," he muttered, a constant refrain. At first, he had blamed everyone around him, if only to survive so much loss. But eventually, the anger had turned inward into a dark resentment, fueled even further by the loss of his arm and it's magical, mechanical replacement.

He squeezed his metallic fist, the piece of machinery responding to emotion.

Perrom stepped over rotting logs, barely missing a sleeping rattlesnake. The snake roused and poked its head up, ready to strike but pulled back when it saw the potential victim. The Gardener's son was not to be harmed. Every creature of every size, fur or feather, knew that rule.

Perrom stopped, listening to the woods. He backed up to a nearby copse of trees and slowly blended into the background, rendering himself invisible. Only the movement of the multiple irises working independently of each other gave him away.

A young buck with a speckled back and silver feathers adorning his growing antlers passed nearby, sniffing at the ground. The silver would slowly turn to gold as he aged. A smaller doe was not far behind him. Perrom watched the pair and felt his breathing slow. "A good omen," he whispered. The reprieve didn't last. A familiar ache returned to his chest, catching in his throat. He lived with it as a constant, sometimes relieved by dreams of Ossonia just outside of his arms that seemed all too real.

The Wood Elf grew restless and slowly emerged, his skin changing from the grey ridges of the nearby bark to his smooth, honey-colored skin. The buck startled, raising his head and stared briefly at Perrom, before turning to trot away, the doe already running ahead. She stopped not too far away, in another open spot where sunshine and tender roots for chewing were more abundant.

Perrom watched the buck stop and nuzzle the doe, the resentment burning his throat. He turned away, scanning the forest. "Focus." He was used to hearing only his voice in short commands, given to help him stay on mission. *Rescue Ossonia, bring her back to me.*

He scanned the area, finally spotting what he had seen yesterday on a run through the woods. A shimmer, barely noticeable, among a cluster of wild red poppies. It was impossible to find it again yesterday in the fading sunlight, but he was sure it was there.

A thin place between this world and the World in Between. The shimmer, where the poppies seemed to blur was the only tell. His heart pounded in his chest. He approached hesitantly, afraid it could somehow disappear if he was too rough or wanted it too badly. He crouched a foot away, watching the shimmer hold its place. Slowly, he raised his left hand, the one he was born with, and reached out, letting the fingertips gently nudge the space.

He rarely let himself use the mechanical right arm.

A gelatinous substance pressed against his fingers, leaving a sticky residue. He could feel his face warm with anticipation. "It's real." He pushed harder, applying steady pressure but the thin wall that separated him from the dreaded way station had almost no further give.

He sat back on his heels and steadied his breathing. Magic always worked better from a calm heart. A basic rule. He gave himself a minute, just letting the sounds of the forest wash over him and the pieces of sunshine reaching him, warm his skin. Something sharp poked at his ribs and he realized it was a feeling of hope. The idea had become unfamiliar. It was not something he let himself indulge in very often. He already had enough sorrow to carry.

"You can do it." A rare plea to himself to believe in the possibilities.

He adjusted slightly, still balancing on his heels and rubbed his one real hand on his other sleeve, warming it up. He reached inside his vest pocket and pulled out a pinch of ginger root, mixed with turmeric and ground birch bark, the dried remains of a mouse's heart and bits of an owl feather. He opened his fingers and let the wind take the grains, spreading them out in a neat, thin line between Perrom and the shimmering poppies.

He held up the hand, palm facing the thin spot and said the words he had practiced so often in the middle of the night. "Return to me what I most cherish. Restore my heart. Replenish my well."

The palm began to glow around the edges, burning

brighter and brighter, emanating the warmth outward toward the thin spot, weakening it just enough.

The shimmer spread out over the flowers, growing larger. Blurry images began to appear, floating back and forth, becoming clearer as an elbow, or a shoulder or a lock of hair. Bodies lost to the other side were pushing against each other, trying to see who was knocking at their door.

It wasn't long before the tangle of bodies pulled back, leaving space. The warmth of the spell was taking hold, searching out what Perrom cherished most.

There was a whoosh and a round thump that sent out a vibration Perrom could feel along his chin, rattling his teeth. He held perfectly still, his hand still hanging in the air, putting out a warmth that began from his heart.

Suddenly, there she was. Her oval face and long, blonde hair filling the space. Her pink mouth in a surprised 'o' and her blue eyes wide with surprise, love and pain in equal measures.

"Perrom."

He heard the word like an echo, the line of powder between them serving as a tuning fork for the sound. He felt a rush of energy move up his body, crashing into his head, but he didn't move. There she was at last, Ossonia. He blinked quickly, his eyes filling with tears.

"Ossonia," he said softly, loud enough to get across the barrier, amplified by the magic powder. Her hand appeared, pressed flat against the divide. Perrom raised his hand and slowly pressed his skin against the outline, feeling the pressure of her hand. "I'm going to get you out." There it was again. Hope stirring inside of him. *Is it possible for so much damage to be repaired? So much pain to be erased?*

Ossonia smiled at the corners of her mouth, her eyes searching his face.

"I swear," said Perrom, nodding his head. "If it's the last good thing I do, with my last breath. I won't leave you in there." He could feel the connection slipping. The magic could only resist the pull of the World in Between for so long. "I love you, Ossonia. Forever."

"I love you too." The echo filled his ears, but he could already hear the words trailing off. Her hand pulled back from the space and her face was growing blurry. "I love you," he shouted. "I will find you! We will be together again."

The shimmer over the poppies shrunk back to its original size and the wind that was always sweeping through the forest picked up the neatly ordered grains of the potion and swept them along, erasing the line.

Perrom sat back on the ground with a thud, still feeling the pressure of Ossonia's hand pressed against his. "She's alive and I can find her," he whispered. His most hopeful sentence in a very long time.

---

The Dryad watched her son from the shadowy confines of the roomy interior inside the old oak tree that stretched far above the others. Its roots were large enough to engulf a tall man and the branches served as a canopy for the saplings below it.

Perrom's mother pressed her palms flat against her chest as she watched Perrom linger. As if Ossonia would magically find a way to reappear just once more for a few seconds. He was motionless, watching the shimmer vibrate for what felt like minutes, and probably was. The Dryad longed to go to him and wrap her arms around him, but she had tried too many times already only to make him retreat further into the forest.

He had even managed to hide from her a few times. Something she thought was impossible till Perrom found a way. No sound, no footstep, no familiar scent she would always know, anywhere. No trace of him and the Dryad had been left to wait till he reappeared on his own again, a few days later. That was when her breath finally returned to her, and she could stop wandering from tree to tree.

Perrom finally rose, still watching the shimmer. The Dryad caught a view of the side of his face and was startled to see his expression had softened from the blank gloom he usually had etched in place. "No," she whispered, worried what the slightest bit of optimism might do to her son, once it was taken away.

Still, she wanted to believe in the impossible, too. "Restore my son. Bring back Ossonia," she whispered to the trees who swayed in response, knowing there was nothing they could do to fulfill her wish.

It was a bit longer before Perrom took a look around as if he was memorizing the spot, and then reluctantly wandered away. Instead of his usual graceful footfalls, each step was noisy and disturbed the smallest of creatures. But no one got in his way. The forest knew and did its best to make room for Perrom and his grief.

The Dryad did her best to do the same, holding her own sorrows close as well.

What she failed to notice, though, was the small tear left

behind in the corner of the shimmer, slowly leaking droplets of ooze and drawing the attention of a darker force that was pleased to see yet another new outlet. Even if the Dryad and Perrom were struggling to gather any kind of optimism and hold onto it, there were other forces that were not having any trouble at all. Things seemed to be coming together nicely, for them.

## CHAPTER NINETEEN

Louie looked at Ronnie, huddled under their table at the entrance to the Dark Market. The Gnome was on his knees in the packed dirt, pulling out different small boxes made of wood or leather, or even metal, searching for a bracelet.

"I don't see it," said Ronnie, poking his head out into the sunshine. "I told you; I think we sold it last week to a bunch of trolls. It could be anywhere by now."

"Leira needs a new bracelet and sooner rather than later. A new brake to her magic. Check again."

Ronnie shaded his eyes. "The last one practically melted. Besides, the bounty hunter takes it off when things get really bad. The very time it should stay put." Ronnie's eyes widened, looking just over Louie's shoulder. "Oh, hey--" The Gnome ducked back under the table without another word.

Louie frowned, slowly turning. After all, it was the Dark Market. It could be anyone, or even anything, armed for a fight. But Louie knew before he even began turning, it was worse. The heavy smell of patchouli gave her away.

"Hello Mom," said Louie, doing his best to sound casual, his face frozen in the same, mild frown. "Aren't you slumming it? Open air markets that let in anyone and never deal in designer anything aren't really your thing."

Liselle was standing in front of his table in a long, dark red silk cowl drawn up over her dark hair. Small, soft hands were clutching the front of the cowl where it opened at her neck. She tilted her chin up toward her tall son. "You're looking well. It's been too long."

"Let's not start right in the middle of a fight, Mom. I like it when we warm up to one. Makes for a longer, more well-rounded visit that can leave us wanting less for another few years."

Liselle pursed her lips, staring at her son. "You get that attitude from your father's side. Is this your new business?" She picked up a small bejeweled box turning it over to read the inscription on the bottom. Blue sparks of electricity stretched out over the box, vibrating her hand. "Children can do that."

Louie took the box from her hands and carefully placed it back on the table. It wasn't helping that she was right. He could feel his mood growing darker.

*Listen to what she has to say.* The sword was speaking to him, rustling in its box under the table, pushing at Ronnie who was still refusing to come out in full view of Liselle. He still had scars that dotted his back from the last time they saw her years ago. The argument had grown to the muttering of spells and wands waved in the air and somehow Ronnie was caught in the middle.

Liselle attempted to look over the edge of the table, but Louie leaned forward, placing his hands firmly on the table, his shoulders hunched, blocking her. "Look, Mother dearest, let's make this easy. Like a business transaction. Less chance of burning down my neighbors' tables. Tell me what you want and if I can sell it to you, I will. Then you can grab the first portal back to Kentucky and we can both work at forgetting each other again."

"How did it get this bad?" Liselle let the cowl drop off her head, her wavy dark hair falling around her shoulders. More than one vendor looked up to see if they knew the remarkable witch. Louie was used to his mother drawing attention. He had even been proud of it, once upon a time.

The question got under his skin. He tapped the table, doing his best not to fire the first verbal jab. "Sometime around when you decided to go back to the dark side. That's my best guess." *Damn, okay, I started it this time. So be it.* "You here to resupply the weapons cache?"

The sword stirred again, banging the box against Ronnie's knee knocking him out from under the table and sliding off the lid. *Listen to what she has to say.*

Louie let out an exasperated sigh and folded his arms over his chest. "Why are you here, Mom? You clearly want something. No one comes to the Dark Market without a need, and you in particular. What does that fortress you call home lack?"

Liselle walked slowly around the table and made a point of straightening her son's collar, glancing down at the sword. "The rumors are true. It's always nice when that happens. A little bit of honesty out there in the world. You have the fabled sword. I'm not surprised it chose you."

"Mom, why? Why are you here?" Louie took both her hands in his, pulling her away from him. "Is it the sword? Do you need my help?"

It happened so fast, Louie didn't have time to react. It was just like his mother, too. To move so gracefully, in one fluid motion that to everyone nearby it was okay, even if her hand was on your wallet or your wand. But this time, her hand was firmly grasping the hilt of the sword, lifting it into the open air.

Liselle didn't get far. The hilt suddenly went from a steely blue to red hot, scalding the palm of her hand. "Damn relic!" The witch let go, letting the sword fall into the dirt and studying the welts already appearing on her pale skin.

Louie felt a mixture of revenge and anger and the need to protect her, only making him angrier but at himself. "The sword's not for sale, and I don't think it likes you."

"Stop being such an obstinate child!" Liselle shook her hand, the lines around her mouth deepening from the pain. "I'm not here for the sword." She spit out the words, pulling a salve out from under the cowl and rubbing it into her hand. It wasn't long before the welts vanished from her hand and Liselle was doing her best to regain her composure. "I'm here to ask for your help."

"There it is. You ever notice you never show up to just say hello and check on me?"

"That goes both ways now that you're a grown wizard."

"He prefers just 'man'," said Ronnie, finally standing and brushing off his knees. He glanced up at Louie who gave him a nod. Their signal to get lost for a while.

Louie waited till Ronnie was gone, wandering into the

tent to look for friends. He kept his lips pressed together, sizing up his mother. *First one talks, loses.* Leira taught him that.

"I can see you're still just as stubborn," said Liselle. "You get that from me." She tried a weary smile. "I have come to ask for your help because you're my son and you're good at what you do. Your other profession. I need to find out if something is true and if it is, what to do about it. Are you willing to listen?"

That was new. Liselle didn't normally care what someone else wanted.

Louie considered saying no, but despite all his efforts at trying to forget his mother, he still cared. It always got him in the end. "What's happened?" he said, ending the silence. "You have an army of dark witches and wizards around you and a fabled dark library. What do I bring to the mess you're in that's unique enough to drag you to another world?"

"Anonymity. Nothing is hunting you." Liselle stared coldly back at him before glancing at the Ogre trying to push his wide girth past her and get into the tent. She brushed a stray lock off her forehead. "But something is definitely hunting me, and all of my kind. Something evil." She held up a hand. "Too easy a joke, even for you. Let it go. There is a new kind of energy that's come into this world and whoever it is – they don't care about destruction, or history, or creating something better."

Louie started to say something but thought better of it. It was too late, though. Liselle saw his hesitation and dipped her chin for a moment, talking to her shoes. "I know what you think of me. None of it good. I suppose in a lot of ways I've earned most of it. But not as much as you want to give me credit." She nervously licked her bottom lip, startling Louie. Liselle never looked like she wasn't sure of what was happening around her. She looked up at her son, her eyes wide. "I made a lot of mistakes with you, but I've always loved you. I'm even proud of you. You don't take shit from anyone. You are your own person." His mother pressed her fingers delicately against her forehead, still looking at him. "You have a kindness that is in your bones. I envy that and it will serve you well. You will always know who you can trust, no matter what. Believe it or not, the Dark Families can operate the same way, most of the time." She waved a hand in the air. "This new entity means to change all that. Nothing will matter. There will be no purpose to anything. Can you imagine that? No endgame beyond destruction."

"What do you want from me?" Louie felt himself wanting to help her, despite everything.

"I want information that could help save us all, or at least most of us, before it's too late. I know you're aligned with Leira Berens. Ask her and tell her the truth if you need to. That your mother wants to know, and why. Surely, she has noticed that something is approaching us that will rewrite everything. Ask her for help, please." She grasped Louie's hand tightly, surprising him. The warmth of her hand made him want to reach out and hug her, feel his mother's embrace, but he didn't dare. Still, he felt the spark of humanity jump across the void, looking for any hidden motives. A nagging fear grew in him when he realized she was telling the truth without embellishments. Even more, she actually loved him.

"I'm glad you have the sword," she whispered to her son. "May it keep you safe, always. Be careful this time, Louie. I know you think you're indestructible but imagine a force that can do something worse than just kill you. Stay on guard because once it knows who you are, it will hunt you too."

The icy tone of her voice made a chill ride down Louie's back. "Are you safe?" he asked, surprised at how much he cared about the answer.

"No, none of us are right now," she said, matter of factly. "But I will fight to my dying breath to make sure we become safe, again."

He was still holding his mother's hand and he felt the spark return an answer to a question he badly wanted to know. She would fight to the end to protect him.

"Let's get this motherfucker," Louie said, quietly. "And get back to our more mundane resentments."

Liselle smiled for the first time. "Like a normal family."

## CHAPTER TWENTY

Leira and Correk stood side by side, their eyes wide, staring at their unexpected visitor. Turner Underwood was standing in their kitchen in aqua blue board shorts and an Hawaiian shirt with pink and green palm trees. His usual cane was replaced with one made of mottled monkeypod wood topped with a silver knob that made Leira smile. "Elegance is always necessary," she said, repeating one of Underwood's favorite sayings.

"Quite right!" he said, tapping the tropical cane against their old wooden floor. "What's wrong, my young Fixer? You act like you're seeing something you've never seen before. A Light Elf from Oriceran who's been a Fixer for months now. Surely, this isn't that surprising?"

Correk scratched the back of his head, amused. "It's strange what can catch you off guard."

"Like a zoo with magical animals for the occupants of this world to gawk at? Yes, I heard about that one. Old Ingram is a frequent flier. He's in need of a good rescue every year about this time. I can mark the season by him. I trust everything turned out as it should."

"However it turned out, that was how it should," said Correk, arching a brow.

Turner let out a short laugh, patting his belly. "Well done!" He settled himself onto a kitchen chair, resting his cane against the wall. "Where is the troll? He's close at hand, I assume."

Everyone looked up at the sound of a tiny car racing along a track just overhead.

"He's nearby," said Leira.

"I've always loved how you have given him more free rein than most bonded magicals will allow. Very wise. Trolls are more like companions or friends and very astute. Strange twist in their magic, that bonding business. Some say it was a curse placed thousands of years ago." Turner threw up his hands, making the palm trees on his shirt sway. "Who's to say?"

"Turner, did you interrupt your retirement someplace warm to come hang out with us in rainy D.C. in our small kitchen?" Leira picked up the nearby open box of Fruit Loops and gave it a shake. "Did you want something to eat. I feel pretty confident the troll didn't take a swim through this box." She looked up in time to see Correk shaking his head behind Turner and put the box down, looking over at her empty bowl. "Well, maybe not this one."

"I'm coming out of retirement to ask for help. Specifically, from you, Leira." He tilted his head in the same way Correk did when there was a magical in trouble. "You know, it never quite goes away. I can still always hear the calls. But, not to worry, I'm not here to take back the mantel of Fixer. Once that is passed, it's for good. No take backs."

Leira saw Correk raise his chin, another tell. "You know why he's here, don't you?"

The old Fixer looked at his replacement and furrowed his brow, rubbing his chin. "That is a relief, actually. I picked the right magical as my successor."

"Somebody want to tell me?" Leira tilted her head, frowning at Correk. "You and I will talk about secrets later."

"Great, I would love to hear any you're keeping from me about cases." Correk crossed his muscled arms over his chest.

Turner laughed, slapping the top of the table. "My favorite people! Well, since I've caused some discord, at least let me make it worth your while. Sit, Leira, sit." He waited till she was at eye level and took one of her hands. Leira felt the magic coiling up her legs and her eyes began to glow. The warmth of Turner's magic jumped along her skin like a rock across a lake, seeking out her energy.

"I'll get right to it." But he hesitated anyway, pausing and smacking his lips together, his face growing somber. "The dark side of the World in Between, it was enhanced during the last great battle. All the coming and going of the living and the dead and the surge of energy that went with it--"

Leira sat back, watching the symbols slowly start to flip, calculating what might come next.

"Interesting little lie detector you have there. I could try and tell you, your choice to let out the Jasper light had nothing to do with any of this." He tapped her forearm, making the symbols jump from a spark of his magic always coursing through him. "But your inner magic would tell you the truth. Never regret your decisions in battle, if you can. We all do the best we can and if we live to tell the tale then all is well. But--" he pointed a stout finger toward the ceiling. "Sometimes, there are unforeseen consequences of a certain magnitude. I have connections on that side of the plane and there is a lot of talk about something new and much more dangerous. No one can say exactly what, but they know enough to fear it."

"Wolfstan Humphrey." Correk let the words slip out, looking straight at Leira.

"What? No, he can't be over there." Leira stood up suddenly, almost knocking over the chair. The mention of his name could still warm her chest instantly with anger. The symbols picked up speed, flipping a little faster. Leira looked down, skimming them quickly. "No," she said, shaking her head.

"It's very possible," said Turner, wearily nodding. "A worthy foe, he saw what was coming at the end of the battle and the devil made a deal with the space that separates the living and the dead. It was convenient timing for him, I'm afraid. The Dark Mist, that lake of misery that seeks you out, has been growing a mind of its own. Not exactly sentient." Turner glanced up at Correk, nodding slowly. "But just enough to be able to see an opportunity. Wolfstan had a particular strength and when brought into the fold, he completed the project."

Leira put her fists on her hips, taking a step back. Her usual battle stance. "The Dark Mist has grown sentient because of Wolfstan Humphrey." She took a slow look around her kitchen, the sound of several small cars racing overhead, her eyes wide. Still, inside she felt calm. At last, she knew what was hunting her. "Something is wrong," she whispered. "Wolfstan Humphrey lives and he's found frenemies."

"And they are planning something." Turner rose out of his chair, taking hold of his cane. "You are now the missing piece of the new plan, I daresay. Your light is a power that can change the balance of power."

"Don't ask this, Turner." Correk shook his head in protest. "Don't use Leira as bait." He worked his jaw, the lines around his eyes standing out. He tapped his chest hard. "We work as a team, together. No one goes out alone in this family."

Turner put out his large hand, resting it heavily on Correk's arm. "Let the bounty hunter speak," he said, in his deep, gravelly voice.

"I get the final decision in this." Leira said it softly but determined. The full weight of her actions on that battlefield were still coming to her, every time she saw the deep pain Correk tried to hide, but she could see it. "I gave you my word that I won't do anything without help, or without reasoning it out."

Correk came and held her firmly by her arms. "None of that may matter this time." His words sounded almost like a plea or a barter. "This thing, this dark tide is a thousand foes blended into one with Wolfstan's evil piloting it. There is so much dark power there." He looked into her eyes and Leira saw the pain flash across his face, again. "No, please," he whispered, resting his forehead against hers. "We can't save the world," he whispered.

Leira felt his pain jump across to her, mixing with her

energy. *I'm sorry, so sorry.* "No, but we can try. It's who we are. We believe in the possibilities." She rested her hands against his chest. "If it's the last good thing we do," she said quietly. "We always try. We aren't the kind who stand by and make others sacrifice. We fight on, together."

Correk shut his eyes, his lips pressed together in a thin line and his long hair falling like a blonde curtain around their faces. "Please be careful," he said, his voice catching.

Turner Underwood cleared his throat, gently tapping his cane. "We need a plan and to gather our own forces. Get the troll. He will be a necessary asset on this one. Every kind of creature out there will need to be an ally if we are to conquer our foe, at last. Then, meet me in my library after your excursion this evening. A lesson with Tess awaits you." Turner slapped Correk gently on the back. "This will not be something the two of you take on, alone. Our entire tribe, from two worlds will stand beside us. I'll see to it. I'll be in touch. Work on the plan and ask Yumfuck what he already knows."

Before Leira could say anything, Turner had tapped his cane hard against the ground and was gone. His voice came to her in an echo meant only for her. *Ask Ariana for help. It's time. You know what to do.* Turner's trump card that was only to be played when things were dire. A shiver went down Leira's spine, ending in the warmth from her old scar and merging into a swirl in her belly.

She kissed Correk hard on the lips, holding his face in her hands. "Turner is right. We will all figure this out."

"I love you, Leira Berens."

"Me too. Every day, all day long, Correk, for at least a hundred more years."

"Not long enough."

Leira smiled. "Hey, can you disappear like that? Is that a Fixer thing or a Turner thing."

Correk laughed, the smile not getting quite to his eyes, but Leira was grateful all the same. "A Turner thing but he promised he'd show me, one of these days."

"And you'll show me, of course." They both laughed and he squeezed his arms around her.

"We will always have things we have to keep to ourselves, but not what matters." Correk's smile slipped from his face. "Not this time. No more holding back, I promise too. We will face what's coming together."

Leira laid her head on his chest and pulled him close so he wouldn't see the look on her face or be able to read the last of the symbols that were already fading from her arms. They had been unable to come up with a future course of action that could be met with any kind of success. *I choose to believe in the possibilities.* She held Correk tighter. *There is no fate. Things can change, especially with magic. Please, let it be true.*

## CHAPTER TWENTY-ONE

"Laura? No wait, Lee-rah? Hold on, hmmm, Leira, I think? Leira, your grande black coffee and chai latte are up." The Starbucks barista snapped a lid on the latte and pushed the cups toward the far edge of the counter. Leira got up to retrieve her order, keeping one eye on her small black backpack sitting in her chair. "Thanks," she said, picking up the black coffee and taking a gulp of the hot liquid before it was cooled. "Manna from heaven," she muttered. A nearby Wizard gave her a wink and raised his cup. Leira could see the telltale gold swirling trail surrounding him. The place was dotted with magicals mixed in among the regular customers. "The real magic elixir," he said. She nodded and carried the order back to her table, putting the latte down and pushing it across, closer to the empty seat.

Leira took another gulp, looking up at the sound of a sudden commotion erupting from the narrow hallway that lead to the bathrooms. An influx of magical commuters were arriving on the underground trains from far flung parts and were pouring out of the hallway. Most of them quickly moved outside, headed to jobs on K Street or in the embassies or Congress. Some stopped to grab coffee, ignoring the usual stares from people who wondered how many people were using those bathrooms. The same thing would happen in another thirty minutes when the next morning express trains pulled up far below.

Leira looked toward the hallway as the last of the commuters emerged, checking her watch. Finally, Ariana came around the corner in a long red wool coat, a healthy distance between the last magicals and herself. Leira smiled, sipping her coffee. Ariana slowly made her way over to the small, round table and carefully arranged herself in the narrow, metal chair. The long coat spread out over the chair revealing a pale grey silk lining.

"Glad you could make it," said Leira. "Chai latte, as requested, whole milk."

"You're surprised to see me? I told you I would be your ally. We have common interests." Ariana removed the lid on her latte and studied the creamy liquid, blowing across the top.

"Explain that part to me again?" Leira sat back in her chair, holding the warm cup close. A crooked smile growing across her face.

"There are dark forces, truly dark forces rising around us." Ariana looked at Leira, arching a brow. "I know what you call us. What everyone calls us. The Dark Families. A little melodramatic. We are really the keepers of our traditions, our magic. The Silver Griffins made up their minds we had no right to keep what was ours."

"Dark magic."

Ariana lifted her cup but paused briefly before slowly taking a sip. "There are those who mistake powerful and effective with dark. You don't need to be one of them. I've seen your handiwork. The same confusion could be said of you."

Leira smiled, setting her cup down and sitting forward, her arms resting comfortably on the wooden tabletop. "It's not about the power, it's about the intention."

"Agreed. We are both looking to protect what we love."

Leira shook her head slowly. "Your family has set out to harm in order to protect. You like to go first, and you tend to go for the throat. Remember something about breeding shifters? I've experienced that firsthand." Leira tapped her chest. "I respond to the attacks." She sat back and picked up her coffee, holding the warm cup against her cheek. A Wizard passed their table and startled when he saw Ariana, hurrying out of the coffee shop. "Your reputation is well known. Even his magic trail tried to get out of your way."

Ariana let out a sigh and took another sip. "You called me here for a reason, Elf. How may I be of service to you?" It was the first time Ariana had smiled, even if it didn't rise all the way to her dark eyes.

Leira's eyes briefly glowed making a customer do a double take before looking in his cup as if there was something special added to the brew. Magic may be out in the open but most still were reluctant to believe in something unseen or out of their reach.

"I need access to the old magic books. The ones you've been hiding in Kentucky."

"Turner Underwood, I presume, filled you in on them. I always suspected he knew exactly where they were." Ariana brushed her hair off her shoulder letting it cascade down her back. "You notice he has never removed them from our possession."

"Your wards make that nearly impossible for the old Fixer, which you already know, and I suspect those are not your family's most treasured books. I'm after the ones even Turner has no idea exist." Leira hesitated, pulling her sleeve down and letting herself relax. The symbols were seeking out the books, calculating the risk. Magic was stirring around her feet. *Not here.* "The ones that can balance light and dark."

The smile faded from Ariana's lips. "Children's fairy tales. There is no such thing."

"There is and we both know it." Leira tapped the table with her finger. "Something even darker is looking for both of us. Something we may not be able to stop this time." She watched Ariana press her lips together, her fingers tightening around her cup. "You're the head of the families. I know you've felt it. I need to see the books. You need to let me through the wards, temporarily. Disguise the route, move the book later. I don't care. I'm not trying to take them away from you. Not this time. I'm asking you to keep your word about helping me. Helping us. We can argue over everything else later."

"You actually sound scared."

"I am smart enough to know when to be afraid and to ask for help. Can you say the same?"

There was another rush of commuters pouring out of the hallway, jockeying around their table to make it to the counter or head outdoors. Ariana waved her well-manicured hand in the air creating a bubble of protection, nearly tripping a few people stumbling over the unseen ward. Leira held out her hand, whispering a spell to help them stay upright, safely making their way to their destination.

Ariana tilted her head to one side. "Always looking to help those who haven't asked you."

"It's my thing. Kind of goes with the whole bounty hunter, former detective thing. Are you going to help?"

"I will give you access for one day for a few hours and that's it. If you don't find anything useful in that time, you're done anyway."

"Full access, Ariana. I want your word."

"I can't give that and you know it. I know the books you seek even if I've never opened them. No one has in thousands of years since the gates to Oriceran were last open. You will be able to view them alone, all of them, but no guarantee on what you will find or how dangerous they may be. Even we have not dared to play with them."

"Good to know you have limits."

"Very few when threatened." Ariana took a look around, finally looking back at Leira. "Silence is golden," she whispered, creating a space around their table. The sound from their voices would drop off not far from their warm bodies and no other sounds would penetrate leaving them in silence. "Something has happened to the World in Between. It's no longer that place that we dread but don't have to notice. The magical purgatory has become a threat to this world, and to Witches and Wizards. Of course I can feel it."

"We found a tear in the fabric between the worlds. A

tear that wasn't closing on its own. Something was guarding it."

Ariana lightly rubbed her chin. "That's impossible, even with magic."

"Not anymore. That thing that oozes through the place has grown a fucking mind. Really, a collective mind, like a beehive or an anthill." It was the first time Leira had ever seen Ariana look worried. Even during the battle with Wolfstan she had stood on the battlefield looking like she expected to win, no matter the odds.

"The prophecy," hissed Ariana, angrily. She jabbed a finger at Leira. "You brought this on us. I knew it. Did you never wonder why we saw you as such a threat?"

"Because you're kind of evil and a little narcissistic? Just a shot in the dark."

"Because you're a Jasper Elf with a spark of humanity. A rare combination that brings in the light at a rate the world can't handle. Darkness will grow just to balance it out. Grow beyond what we can contain or control. You have always been the threat to the rest of us, Leira Berens. Why do you think so many different kinds of magicals banded together to wipe out your kind so long ago?" Ariana got up, breaking the spell around them. The noise of early morning rushed back into their space.

Leira sat back, steadying her breathing. *I need her to help. Fuck me.* "What prophecy, Ariana?"

Ariana leaned closer, whispering the words with a hint of menace to her voice. "It's one of the oldest. Before the seer's time, even. That someday, a light would come that could change the world." Ariana stood up, gathering her coat around her as if a cold wind had found her inside the

Starbucks. "Or destroy it. Come to the estate tonight. Bring no one else, including that troll, or you'll be turned away. The wards will only let in you and only for a few hours." She walked away, not waiting for a response, heading for the hallway and the hidden entrance to the trains.

---

"An ancient prophecy. That would have been helpful to mention, Turner."

"It wasn't evident that you are the light that the prophecy foretold. It's still not." Turner Underwood's booming voice echoed against the wood paneling. He stood in his library in a silk robe, balancing his hands on his favorite cane. The one with a silver falcon as a handle. The edges of the falcon's feathers were worn smooth from so many years of handling.

"Okay, then why not tell me?" Leira was in her tall boots, jeans and leather jacket. Ready for anything. The symbols were flipping over and over on her arms and her eyes were aglow. She was asking the same question over and over again but so far, there was no answer. *Am I the threat to everyone?*

"This is why not," he bellowed. Turner tapped his cane hard on the floor. "No, you are not a threat to anyone except those who have found their way onto a bounty hunter's list," he said sternly, startling Leira. He held up his hand to fend off her next question. "I don't have to read minds. I know you well enough."

"It is creepy how you do that. Is Correk going to get like that someday?"

"With any luck. Take this seriously, Leira. Look this dead in the face."

"Poor choice of words."

"Accurate choice of words. It doesn't matter if the darkness is fulfilling a myth or is hunting you for some other reason. It's still hunting with intent."

"Then take me to Tess, before I see the books. Please. A short cut. You have to have one. All those rooms that exist on another plane."

"I hear your lessons are going well." He tapped the side of his nose. "Those rooms are not stable enough for holding Tess. Her powers would make them even less stable and bringing her out in the open is even more risky. I can get you a few minutes in this library with the seer, but that's it. Then I return her to safekeeping, for all our sakes."

"That will do."

The smell of sage filled the room and Leira turned quickly, recognizing the scent, not sure what to expect. Tess was perched on the chair behind Turner's desk. Her small frame was dwarfed by the bookcases behind her. "Then we had better make it quick," she said, her milky eyes moving around the room as if she was taking in everything. Her long grey hair was tied up neatly in a twist, fastened to the back of her head with a silver clip.

"How did you do that? There wasn't a sound."

Tess laughed and clapped her small hands together. "I've had thousands of years to practice. Who do you think taught this young man? Although he still has a few lessons to learn."

Leira gave a crooked smile despite the magic still

roiling inside of her, demanding attention. Turner let out a short cough giving the Persian carpet light taps with his cane. He sat himself down in a leather chair and gestured to Leira, tilting his head. "You only have a few minutes. Make them count."

"Please tell me about the prophecy that the light will draw in the darkness. Am I the light that could destroy this world?" Leira stayed on the far side of the desk, holding her breath. She could feel her magic going out ahead of her, circling around Tess, looking for answers.

The old seer's cheeks warmed in response turning a bright pink. She rocked gently back and forth, her feet swinging just above the floor. She began humming softly, closing her eyes. Leira opened her mouth to say something, but Turner drew his thick eyebrows together, shaking his head. "Wait," he whispered. "You asked your question already."

The minutes ticked by as Leira stood quietly, waiting. *This is part of the new magic. Patience. Good luck with that.*

Finally, the seer's eyes popped open. She took in a deep breath and turned her face toward Leira, lifting her chin. "The light can never be the cause of destruction. Never. It's a creative force for good. However," she said, reaching out for the desk and bracing her hands against the edge, "remember two things. Light is not everything. It's essential but only part of the answer." Tess held up two fingers. "And darkness can invade anything and dim its power. Anything at all, no matter how powerful. Beware of magic that twists nature into a mirror image of itself. Similar but so different, and dangerous. Trust the path and keep learning to work with the magic. Remember, it's a conversation."

A pen rolled off the desk, landing at Leira's feet. She bent down to get it and straightened up, not completely surprised to find the chair empty.

"I've noticed Tess loves a dramatic exit," said Leira, putting the pen down. "I didn't get an answer to my question."

"I think you did. Enough of one at least. You want to know the outcome as well. A different request. It's why those symbols are searching for you. That's the conversation you're having with the magic that can't be answered."

"Do you think Tess knows the outcome?"

"Not at all. That would mean we all live by fate. Every time you make a new decision, what lies ahead changes. Listen to what Tess actually said to you and heed her words. Beware of power that would dim your light and work with it." He tightened the belt around his robe. "Aren't you late for a meeting? Tell Ariana I said hello." The retired Fixer circled a hand over his head, opening a portal. Leira recognized the green field of Kentucky and the house in the distance.

"I take it, it's time for me to go."

"Past time. I have a date and I need to get ready."

Leira raised her eyebrows and smiled, stepping through the portal. "Enjoy your retirement," she said, as the portal began to close.

"I always do."

## CHAPTER TWENTY-TWO

The assistant manager of the Georgia Avenue McDonald's held Yumfuck up by the back of his blue cape. The troll's furry chest was covered in special sauce and tiny bits of lettuce and burger and his cheeks were still stuffed full. A half-eaten burger was on the floor, the pieces scattered. Tiny bite marks made a track through the middle of it.

"Read the sign," said the skinny teenager. He shook the troll a little and pointed with a wiry arm at the sign. His blue, short-sleeved shirt hung on his body, the collar standing out from his neck and narrow head. A neatly pinned white name tag had *Barry* printed in black letters across it.

The nearby sign read, *No trolls, no gnomes, no dwarves*, hand printed and laminated.

The troll licked the fur around his mouth while waving his arms as if he was swimming through the air till he turned enough to get a good look at Barry. "Seems judgy," he squeaked. "My Yelp review will reflect the service."

Barry let go of the troll in frustration, dropping him from a height, but the troll easily caught on to the front of Barry's neatly pressed shirt, scampering down and leaving greasy paw prints in his wake. He scooped up the remains of the patty, easily missing Barry's shoe that was trying to squash him, running away with the burger held high overhead.

It wasn't the first time the two had tangled. Two weeks ago, Barry had found Yumfuck swimming through the new batch of fries warming under the lamp. His fur twinkled in the light from the bits of salt clinging to his fur.

Each time, Yumfuck managed to evade capture, till today. The fried apple pie slowed him down and left him feeling a little food drunk. He wasn't moving quite as fast. He was panting from the effort of carrying the burger and dodging the feet. Customers leaned over the counter, cheering on the troll.

"Look at him go!"

"It's a rat running on two feet!"

"No, it's a troll. Look at the hair."

"Don't rescue it. Then he's yours for life."

"How do you know it's a boy?"

"Oooh, it's making a break for the kitchen."

"A dollar he gets away clean."

"I'll take that bet."

Yumfuck bit at the burger dangling over his head, lessening the load, the grease dripping on his forehead. He made a sharp right turn, picking up speed and threw the burger slightly ahead, using it as an oily slide toward the exit.

But the assistant manager was faster. Barry scooped

him up, marching back toward the registers. The customers let up a collective howl, booing Barry who stopped and stared at them all. Some had out phones, capturing everything. Barry hung his head for a moment and then lifted Yumfuck just in front of his face, whispering to him. "Listen, little dude. I need this job and you're making that harder. I can't have you running through here, stealing food."

"Borrowing."

"It's not borrowing if you eat it, no matter how it comes out later." Barry pressed his eyes shut for a moment. "I don't even want to think about that." He opened his eyes and put his nose even closer to the troll's, ignoring the hooting and yelling from in front of the counter. "I'll make you a deal. You can work off what you owe, and I'll throw in a free meal each shift. No snacking on the food when you're at the register. After your balance is paid, I can pay you in food."

Yumfuck reached out and grabbed Barry's nose between his paws, kissing the end with a loud smack. "Deal. I've got a few more friends if you need some more--"

"No friends!" Barry's voice went up an octave, breaking into a squeak on the word 'friends'. "If you bring in other trolls, the deal is off."

Yumfuck shrugged, holding out his paws. "You got me, Barry. It's a deal. Where do we start?"

---

It wasn't long before Yumfuck was thoroughly washed in dish soap to remove the grease, rinsed and wrung out and was wearing a tiny paper hat, with a name tag that read, YTT. The small troll was standing on the base of the microphone at the drive through. He stood on the red button, leaning back to yell into the mic, "Welcome to McDonald's. How can we be of service?"

"How can we help you," said fifteen-year-old Jimmy, his eyes half closed with boredom. "It's how can we help you. I don't know that we're trying to be of service."

"I'll take two Happy Meals and a number two super-sized. No ice in the Coke," came the female voice through the speaker.

Yumfuck bounced from the mic to the cash register, leaping from button to button to put in the order.

"Not bad," said Jimmy, wrinkling his forehead with surprise. "I didn't get it that fast my first day." Yumfuck held up his paw. "Don't leave me hanging, Jimmy."

The teenager high-fived the troll, laughing as a white Chevy Tahoe SUV pulled around to the window. The troll made his way to the ledge, pushing open the window and waving at the startled driver. "Well, hello there and welcome to the golden arches! Your day going okay? My name is Yumfuck Tiberius Troll. This is my first day," he said, pushing out his chest a little and curling his tiny paws on his hips. The driver stared back at him, her mouth hanging open. Yumfuck took it as encouragement.

"I like your order. I'm partial to anything that comes with fries, although that special sauce can kick some ass. Maybe someday the toy in a Happy Meal will look like me." He stood up straighter, grinning, his tiny, pointed teeth showing. Jimmy came to the window and leaned around the troll, handing the woman a full white paper bag and her sodas in a cardboard drink tray. The woman took the food without taking her eyes off the troll. She rolled up her window and began to drive away as the troll held out his arm and cheerily yelled, "Aloha motherfucker, come again!" The troll scurried back inside and stood on the mic stand. "Is it time for our dinner break yet?"

"Little guy," said Jimmy, "you are going to be a legend in this place."

## CHAPTER TWENTY-THREE

Leira walked through the tall grass, making her way toward the house. Large black Labradors met her halfway, barking and baring their teeth. Leira thought about lighting up tiny fireballs to ward them off but instead asked the magic running down her spine for help. "What I want to say is, calm the fuck down." She was speaking in a low voice to the dogs, but it was having no effect. "Nope, nope, I'm learning new tricks. I can do things differently." She could feel the flow of magic moving toward the forefront, waiting for her response. "Okay, I can do this magic. Let's work together," she muttered, "Calm the dogs and turn them back."

She felt the energy roll out in front of her, a slight tug at her waist. The glittering trail started out green fading into the grass and gradually turned grey, then purple. "That's new."

The dogs stopped as the magic drew near, sensing a change in the atmosphere around them, but they kept barking even louder, attempting to block Leira's path.

"Have a conversation." Leira let herself relax, licking her lips and calmly walking forward. The palms of her hands itched. "There's a simple fix. A few tiny fireballs would take care of this." The magic momentarily halted as if it was turning back to see if she meant it. "Nope, we are learning to do things differently. Focus. Relax."

The strands of magic picked up speed again, turning in circles, coiling in on itself while still making progress. Eventually the pulsing light, visible only to Leira, reached the dogs, rolling in waves around them, ruffling their fur and weaving around their bodies till they laid down in the grass, panting. The air crackled and sparked.

"Nicely done." Ariana stepped out of the shadows; her long hair tied back in a black velvet ribbon in a defense against the wind blowing across the grassland. "I thought for sure you were going to leave a burn mark across my grass."

"No need. Your dogs are pretty easy going."

"They are Oriceran dogs who are trained for hunting. Easygoing is not in their nature. Stopping visitors by any means necessary is their normal take on a situation. No troll?"

"He was busy. I've chosen to trust you, Ariana. Don't prove me wrong."

"You are not the same magical who stormed the house. Something has changed." Ariana stopped and turned back toward the house. "Follow me and stay close. Not everyone is happy you've been allowed on the grounds." She turned and looked back over her shoulder. "But don't worry, you're safe. I've seen to it."

"Never crossed my mind." Leira watched the strands of

her magic dance out in front of Ariana, making their way to the house ahead of them. Ariana made a path toward the right of the property making her way toward the stables and the entrance that once had wolves pouring out of it, meant to tear Leira apart. Leira did her best to shake off the memories and caught up with Ariana, looking up at the new house, catching a glimpse of an older Wizard watching from an upstairs window.

"That's Uncle Felix. I believe you two have met under different circumstances," said Ariana without looking up. She waved a hand in his general direction. "My dear Uncle is having feelings about our alliance. Ignore him. I often do."

Leira passed over the ground where her partner, Hagan almost died. The scar on her belly warmed. The first hint of anger stirring inside of her. *Not this time. Not today at least.*

They came to a heavy wooden door set into a stone arch behind the stables. Ariana flicked her hand, unfurling her fingers and the door opened with a whoosh, pressing back against the large, limestone blocks. Leira followed behind her at a short distance, feeling an eerie sense of having traveled this way before, only it was just her magic that had swirled down the steps.

Every tall stone stair, the dark mineral stains streaked along the walls, and even the different stalls deep in the earth were familiar to her. She knew exactly where to step and at the bottom when they reached a trio of different hallways, she turned to the right almost overtaking the Witch.

Ariana stopped abruptly, taking a long look at Leira. "You've been here before? That's impossible."

Leira felt Ariana's magic reach out to touch her before she saw the deep black trail of magic skimming along the surface of her skin. Instead of resisting, she felt the urge from a more powerful, expansive source, emerging from every direction.

The nearby tall oaks nodded in cooperation and the wind swirled along the top of the grass, offering its power.

The new energy was flowing in from everywhere, curious to see if the black, shimmering magic would work with hers in cooperation. Combine all the magic.

But the dark smooth stream resisted, rupturing into tiny marbles that fell to the ground, bouncing a moment before dissipating into steam. Ariana's eyes widened in disbelief. "You've changed, Bounty Hunter and I'm not sure I like it. No one turns away my magic."

"No one did this time either." *The real power is in cooperation. I'm beginning to get it Tess. No wards are needed if I stop fighting and work with nature.* The Jasper Elf felt a rush of excitement. *I can do this. We can finally stop Wolfstan.*

Ariana whispered a spell too quietly to be heard and made the shape of a square with her hands, blowing in the center.

*Oof.* Leira's back slammed against the stone wall, knocking the breath out of her. She sucked in air, a fireball appearing in her hand and the anger finally taking root. The natural force stepped back and her own magic surged forward ready to fight. Her eyes glowed and her jaw was set.

Ariana gave the cold smile again. "Much better. This

Leira I know well." Ariana turned to go, pulling out a slender brass key. "You are powerful, but you have a temper, Leira Berens. Perhaps you can learn a thing or two from me."

Leira let the fireball extinguish leaving only a trace of pale grey ash in her palm. There was a hollow feeling in her chest where the natural magic had been swimming. "Lesson learned," she muttered. "Shake it off." She caught up with Ariana, the heels of her boots clicking along the stones. The Witch waved her arm in front of a stone wall making it shimmer and passed through without hesitation.

Leira followed, finding herself in a narrower tunnel lit by torches anchored into the walls over her head. Her shoulders barely fit and there was a strong smell of brine. Ariana was already heading down another set of stairs that ended in another wall that stretched up several hundred feet. Another wave of her arm and the wall shimmered, giving way. "Are you coming? The ward won't step back for long." Ariana curled a finger in Leira's direction. "Now or never. You can go back anytime."

"I like to finish what I start." Leira came down the stairs quickly to catch up, passing through the barrier just behind Ariana. "Where are we?"

"Don't you recognize it? Let me help you. *Illuminata*," she whispered, lighting the small room dug out of the limestone. The walls were inset with shelves stacked with books that went back for three layers. More torches lined the outside going up the wall. A small desk was built into the wall with a neat stack of small, bound books piled on top of it.

"What is happening?" Leira instinctively put out her

arms, ready to fall. Beneath their feet the stone was beginning to turn opaque, revealing a bustling world far beneath them, stretching down hundreds of feet.

"The train system," whispered Leira in surprise. Just beneath them, Leira could see a hazy image of commuters making their way down wooden stairs going in different directions headed toward shiny red rail cars far below, steam rising out of them. She could barely make out the different signs where the staircases branched off of each other halfway down, pointing toward Texas, and another pointing toward Alabama or New York.

She slid her feet over the surface to see if it was still solid. "Just like the Oriceran castle."

"Yes, of course it is. Simple spells. This one, though, comes with a twist." Ariana tapped the ground with her heel causing the images to glow and then fade till it was only a stone floor again. "The Silver Griffins put in so many wards over the years to prevent destruction or detection that it has the added bonus of protecting us as well. I'm not sure they ever realized they helped us create the perfect safe room. Of course, how would they? You don't find what you're not seeking."

"That smell, that's like the sea, what is it? We're landlocked here."

"For another meeting, if all goes well with this one. You don't get every secret today. Only the ones you seek. How to defeat the menace in the World in Between. Go on, take a look. You don't have a lot of time. Uncle Felix will only tolerate your presence for a while. Don't worry, no one else in the families know of this room, not even my uncle. But you will need to go back to the grassy area to open a portal home. It will bother him that he can't detect your presence here anymore."

Leira walked across the floor, feeling the hum of energy rising up from the activity below them. She slid into the seat, twisting back to look at Ariana. "Thank you, I mean it."

"I don't suppose you want me reading over your shoulder?" Ariana leaned into the wall, an arm disappearing through the stone. "The wards are set to let you go if you leave within your three-hour time limit. Don't test me. We have an alliance but not a friendship and I have other things to do. Overstay your welcome and it may be a while before I check this room again."

Leira stared at her with Hagan's favorite dead fish look. "Understood. Hang around too long and I become the official crypt keeper. I've set my watch with plenty of time to spare."

"Be clear of the entire stables, not just this path down. Uncle Felix can get to you in the stables, and he won't hold back. He has a few unfortunate talents of his own." Ariana stepped back, sinking into the wall and was gone.

"What is it with the magicals around me? No one can just say goodbye when they leave." Leira swiveled in the seat, slowly resting a hand on the top book. "Mmmm, you have a nice little rumble of magic." She picked up the book and read the spine. "A Study on Portals." The small book was bound in blue woven cloth with the title stamped in gold letters on the front. It opened stiffly as if it was never read but had no signs of dust or neglect.

A prickle of energy danced across the back of Leira's neck making the hairs stand on end. "This place is creepy on steroids." She turned the first page watching the letters appear. "I haven't seen this kind of lettering in a while. The Gnomes wrote this book." The energy sparked again, pushing at her shoulders and racing around her chest, zinging her old scar and rising up to her throat. *Something is wrong.* "Really wrong. Ariana, you bitch, what have you done?"

The words on the page began to blur, blending together into an inky smear that sizzled when it came into contact with Leira's skin. She pulled her hand back, a sudden pounding in her head and an acrid smell in her nose making it hard to take a deep breath. "Great, I invited myself into their bear trap. Hagan would not be happy with me."

The briny smell returned, this time filling the space. Leira tried to rise out of the chair and search for the door, but she fell to her knees, lightheaded, her hands slamming onto the stone floor. The inky stains on her fingers made contact with the stone, her fingers pushing through the floor as if it were a porous sponge. "This can't be good. Please don't tell me this is my final resting place. Correk. Correk," she repeated, willing herself to put two thoughts together. "I broke my word. I was too busy worrying about a different threat."

The soft part of the floor widened in a circle, threatening to take over the room as Leira crawled backward toward the wall and an exit. The smell of saltwater increased as a tear opened in the floor just under the desk, pulling in the chair. The books fell to the floor, scattering and Leira lunged forward taking a chance and grabbing three of the books, pushing them inside her jacket.

*Rip!* The tear became larger, and an ooze crept out of the far corner.

"Fuck me," swore Leira, trying to stand and crawl back against the wall again. "The Dark fucking Mist, even here. Ariana, how did you do this? What am I up against?"

She felt her back press against solid rock, no give and no opening. "I did this to myself. I came alone. Correk, will you even know what happened?" Tears filled her eyes, but she wiped them away. "Not going out like this." Leira shut her eyes even as the dark tide slowly swept toward her. "Breathe. Ask for help now." She called out to the first two faces that appeared to her. "Mom, Nana, help me. I can't do this alone. Please, find me."

She opened her eyes to watch the tide encroach upon her. Just at the edges of the tear in the veil between the worlds she could see through to the train station below her. "Two worlds so close together." Leira wanted to reach out to the glow from the station, but she looked straight ahead at the Dark Mist. "I want to see it coming. I'm not going into that slime without a fight, come what may. Ossonia, we may see each other again, at last."

The Dark Mist bubbled over the floor, darkening the view into the bright world beneath. *Sizzle, pop!* It halted abruptly, rippling backward. Something was blocking its path and melting the edges.

"Mom! Nana! You heard me." Relief poured through Leira. She pressed her back against the wall, forcing herself to stand, as she watched the sparkling streams of green and purple swirl together, pushing back the threat.

The stream split in two, one half curling back toward Leira and passing directly through her, out her back and blending into the stone wall before bouncing back, unable to break off the ward. The smell of sea water grew stronger, and the Dark Mist was splashing up against the walls. Bodies of dead magicals began to take shape, rising out of the thick goo, moaning and reaching their arms out toward Leira.

*Reach inside yourself, daughter. Believe.*

It was her mother's voice echoing in the chamber. Stern and clear, demanding she pay attention.

*Believe. Use all the magic around you, including us. Pay no attention to the tide. Your power will go to wherever you put your attention. Trust me. Let the doubt go.*

Leira felt the warmth of Eireka and Mara's magic surrounding her. She let go of the regret she was holding onto and let herself fall backward into the stream. Her head thumped against the wall even as she blended in with her own energy, setting an intention. *Whatever is out there in everything that lives, help me, please.*

Her magic went out ahead of her, announcing its presence, seeking assistance.

The wind stirred in the treetops and newly formed acorns fell in a shower as energy stirred from every direction answering the request. Magic came from everywhere on the estate, sliding across the grounds, unseen even by the Witches and Wizards just inside the house. Although many suddenly looked up, feeling a change in the air pressure and wondering if there was a storm forming in the clouds overhead.

The magic easily slid past the wards, leaving them undisturbed and sounding no alarms. It came down the stairs and through the two walls, wrapping itself around

Leira and pulling her back just as the Dark Mist reached her boot, melting the edge of her heel. The hands of the dead magicals reached out, desperate and trying to grasp at anything.

But nature had answered Leira's request and was allowing the three women's energy to combine and blend in, pulling Leira gently back through the wall, immediately closing behind her. The Dark Mist splashed up against the impenetrable wall, the dead beating their heads against the stone. Just as suddenly, it pulled back in a whoosh, seeping through the cracks and back through the tear, leaving the room quiet once more.

Leira was on the other side, keeping her breathing steady, letting go of any anger or revenge as she worked her way up the stairs and to the next wall.

"Trust," she muttered. "Everything has to work together in nature." She repeated Tess's lesson, keeping herself calm. Her mother's energy rubbed along her back and gently around her neck. "Thanks, Mom." Leira took in a slow, even breath as she got to the wall, closing her eyes and trusting the magic as she fell forward.

She emerged on the other side, her knees banging against the hard ground and her hands bruising against the hard pebbles mixed into the dirt. Darkness had fallen and the night sky was filled with stars.

The books tucked into her jacket shifted, a corner pressing into her ribs. "Keep breathing. Come on, you can do this. Stand, already!"

Leira pushed herself to her feet, running as best she could through the winding pathway past the old cells where the shifters were held. She saw the old room where

Matthew was held, the rusting shackles resting on the ground. "Let it go, for now." She let out an even breath, still moving, the muscles in her legs remembering what it was like to run. "Nature does not know right or wrong, only consequences. No room for revenge."

She got to the last door and found it open, slowing down to let her magic get out of there first. The magic peeked around the corner and saw the lone figure outside.

"Ariana." A hint of anger sparked in her chest, and she felt the forces of nature slowly and gently draw back. She couldn't hold onto the calm anymore and the added power left her. "Not as easy as it doesn't look," she muttered stepping into the sunshine of the courtyard.

Ariana was standing in the center, her arms crossed over her chest. "You found your way out, I see."

"No thanks to you, Witch." The magical force of nature had receded. There was no need to hold back her fury any longer. A fireball appeared in her hand, ready to go. "You tried to kill me, and with the Dark Mist. Are you crazier than your predecessor?"

Ariana's pale, smooth forehead wrinkled. "The Dark Mist?" She pursed her lips briefly. "Did the thin air or the close quarters get to you? The Dark Mist can't get into that room. No portal can open down there. That's why I let you look at the books in there. No chance you would somehow destroy more of our home, again."

Leira pushed past Ariana, determined to get to the fields, and home. "Well, you're wrong again, and I don't believe you. The Dark Mist was there in all its glory. But wait, there's more," said Leira, doing annoyed jazz hands, still marching toward the fields. "Zombie magicals mixed in for fun."

"Leira, stop! I didn't do that. Stop!"

There was something in Ariana's voice, an uncharacteristic plea, that made Leira stop and turn back. She was almost to the grass, but she ran back enough to hear Ariana. "That's impossible. How did that thing find me all the way down there in your batshit cave?" Leira's eyes widened. "It was that book you left on top. You wanted me to fail, just not in such a big way."

Ariana clenched her fists. "Not fail entirely. I wanted to help you and leave you with a message. We are not your convenience store where you can stop in and get what you need and then desert us."

"When have you ever asked for anything?" Leira took a step toward Ariana. "And now your arrogance has threatened your home. You are no different, Ariana. Once again, I'm not the big threat you want to believe I am, you are."

"You might want to go check on your precious room. It may be gone by now and rumor has it the other side has figured out how to keep tears open and come and go at will. Looks like you have new tenants. Don't worry though, they're all dead and they don't eat much but they kind of stink."

The color drained from Ariana's face. "Those books you took, take care of them," she said hurriedly, as she turned and ran into the building.

"That was the plan." Leira didn't waste any time and turned to run but was stopped by another familiar figure. "Uncle Felix, were your feelings hurt you were left out of the party?"

"Leaving already? I see your escort has abandoned you."

"She went to welcome your new guests. You'll love them."

A look of confusion passed across Uncle Felix but he quickly returned to his task at hand. "You're a trespasser. I'm well within my rights to dispatch you."

"Fine, have it your way. I've been itching to do this all night, anyway." Fireballs appeared in her hands and she prepared to throw them, still asking for Mara and Eireka's help. Her bones ached and her head was still foggy, but she wasn't going down without taking a piece of him with her.

A familiar roar echoed loudly from the distance, catching both of them off guard. Uncle Felix startled, his mouth falling open as he turned in time to see an eight-foot Yumfuck lumbering toward him at a gallop. The edges of his lips were still blue. Correk was running next to him, already loading an arrow in his bow.

Uncle Felix waved his arms in large circles, showering them all with small drops of fire, but the Fixer was ready. He shot an arrow, letting it arc over the top of the fiery rain, releasing a curtain of purple raindrops that doused the fire. The few that reached the troll were quickly stamped out, barely singeing his fur.

Leira patted her hair, shaking off the rest.

Uncle Felix licked his lips nervously, choosing to make a break for it and run toward the relative safety of the large house, calling for help.

Correk caught up to Leira and enveloped her in his arms, pushing her head against his chest. "The troll turned blue. Then Mara's energy showed up, pulling me toward you."

"Of course she did," said Leira, sliding her arms around his waist. Yumfuck leaned back, letting out another roar, a warning to anyone nearby before squeezing his arms around the pair in front of him.

"Why does Yumfuck smell like old french fries?"

"Come on, let's go." He took Leira's hand, pulling her toward the grassy fields and beyond the wards. "I think he got a job."

"I said I got a job," said the troll, keeping his large stature and running alongside them. "I'm flipping burgers."

"Am I still hallucinating?"

"Why do you smell like old fish?"

"A short and terrible story. The Dark Mist has found the Dark Families. A match like no other."

Other Witches and Wizards came pouring out of the main house, pointing to Leira, Correk and the troll and shouting different orders. Correk let go of Leira's hand to load another arrow. "We need to get out of here. Did Ariana break her word?"

"No, I think. I can't be sure. I'm not sure she's okay, either. She went back to confront that slimy blob."

Correk looked back toward the stables and the heavy wooden door in the distance. "I would not wish that on anyone but Wolfstan Humphrey."

"Me either. Help me." Leira started running back toward the stables. Correk grunted in anger but took his bow off his shoulder and began firing arrows over the heads of the Witches and Wizards, pushing them away from the house and their hiding places. The troll galloped after Leira, dropping to all four paws. The few Wizards who dared to follow them were met with a swipe of his paw and drew back to a safer distance.

Leira ran into the stone structure, down the passageways, sliding on the pebbles and pushing against a wall to stay upright, turning the corner past the first cells.

She got to the first wall, not sure what to do just as Ariana came bursting through, a look of panic across her face. Leira pulled her further away from the wall, the books threatening to spill out of her coat.

Ariana pulled back, looking at Leira in surprise. "You came back for me."

"No thanks to your Uncle and assorted third cousins. You still have all your parts?"

"So far, and I managed to close the tear but the small library may be lost. There were a few ancient, irreplaceable texts in there."

"How did you close the tear."

"Check the books you took. It's in one of them." Ariana pinched the bridge of her nose. "Go, get out of here. I've done all I can for you but remember this when we need help. That day will come."

"Maybe soon," said the troll. "Trouble is getting closer."

"Leira, get off of my lawn. Uncle Felix will be whipping everyone into some kind of frenzy. I can stop them but --"

"You don't want to create bad blood. I'm going and thank you," said Leira, tapping the hidden books. She came out of the clearing ready for trouble. An older witch with silver hair in braids pinned across the top of her head was holding her wand aloft, muttering spells. Dust pricked at Leira's skin, getting in her eyes and making it difficult to see Correk. She put an arm over her eyes and rolled out a line of fireballs that created a wall of clear, blue white-hot fire. "That should keep the Witch busy for a minute."

Leira and the troll took off running, keeping the house to their back to guide them through the remains of the dust storm.

They passed through the last ward, the tug pulling at them as they stepped over it, the air finally clearing. Correk opened a portal to their kitchen, but Leira pulled him back, checking the corners. "I need to be sure. No holes in the portal." She stepped through into the calm and safety of their townhouse as the troll shrunk down and passed through, Correk close behind them. He quickly closed the portal as a fireball sailed in their direction. It was too late though and passed through the air, lighting up part of the field.

Leira sat down in one of the chairs, inspecting her boot and pulling the books out of her coat. "I did come away with a few door prizes. Ancient books that supposedly know something about the World in Between. Maybe even the Dark Mist."

"So dangerous books."

"Necessary reading material." Leira scooped them up, holding them close. "I know your job as Fixer is to take just this kind of thing away from magicals."

"Because they regularly blow themselves up, start fires, open weird portals and even morph a body part or two."

"We need this information."

"Also in the top ten of justifications."

"The other side won't stop coming for us and now they have magical zombies and Wolfstan Humphrey. We have no idea what their source of magic is or how to stop them. Even Turner Underwood is worried."

Correk put his bow and quiver away in the pantry. "All true but you are choosing to use magic that distorts nature. There are always consequences."

"Not use, learn more about it."

"What would Tess say?"

"Dark magic distorts natural magic and weakens it with unforeseen consequences. Then she'd disappear in a puff of smoke. I need to know, Correk." The troll crawled up her pant leg and disappeared into her coat pocket, curling into a ball. It wasn't long before he was softly snoring. "Does Yumfuck really have a job?"

"Trolls don't lie, just like Willens. Somehow, he's got a job where there's a lot of fast food. I expect to be breaking up some mayhem as the Fixer by his third shift."

"I saw the old cells where they held Matthew and the other shifters. A special kind of stupid evil clings to that place."

And you want to use their magic."

"Just learn about it, I promise. We need an edge and so far, I have no idea where it's going to come from. Maybe one of these books can at least tell us what makes up the Dark Mist. That would be a place to start." Leira stood up, stretching her arms over her head. "Do you ever get distress calls from the Dark Family members?"

"Are you worried about Ariana? She's more powerful than she lets others know. But yes, I've saved some of them a few times. Repeat customers. Dark magic generally has a stupid ending."

"Maybe this time it can have a few helpful clues."

## CHAPTER TWENTY-FOUR

Patsy and Lois entered the Carousel Lounge, passing by the tall stuffed giraffe and into a thicket of former agents wandering about the bar like they weren't sure what to do with themselves. A Witch near the entrance turned and saw the pair, letting out an audible gasp. "You're alive!" She shook her hands over her head, releasing gold dust that rose to the ceiling, passing over everyone's head before falling in a light mist.

"Great, magical confetti," whispered Lois. "Uncle Petie won't get rid of that for months. Keep your mouth shut, Patsy. The stuff is bitter."

"That was a go to for you back in the day. Becoming head of the Silver Griffins has made you a stickler for your own rules."

Lois arched an eyebrow at Patsy but didn't argue the point. "I need to find Uncle Petie. Come stand next to me when we begin."

"Roger that," said Patsy with a sharp salute.

"Don't start treating me like the Feds we used to work for. I'm still me."

"Kind of true. What? I won't tell anyone. You like being the boss. Through hellfire and actual brimstone you've earned it. Enjoy it! I would be and there would always be an assistant with snacks following us everywhere." She gently gave Lois a nudge. "Go on, find Uncle Petie and let's get this show started. They have food in this place?"

Lois just stared at Patsy without answering, finally giving a small shake of her head and walking away without answering.

"Simple question," said Patsy, scanning the bar top for a menu. Witches and Wizards were pointing at her, whispering. A tall, heavyset Witch even came close enough to squeeze Patsy's arm and stare closely into her eyes, muttering an authentication spell. Gold flecks appeared in Patsy's irises, melting into the background just as quickly.

"Yeah, it's really her. I owe you a dollar. They're not dead," said the Witch in a low, gravelly voice, lumbering back to her small knot of friends.

"Okay, hello to you too. Would have thought there'd be a little more relief coming from the crowd." Patsy eyed the pink, papier mâché elephant near the bandstand inside the Carousel Lounge. "You have to admire someone who commits to a theme."

The cook, a well-muscled Gnome named Harry sidled up to Patsy, wiping his hands on a grease-stained nubby white hand towel. "That's only the start for Uncle Petie. You have no idea. Wait till Uncle Petie locks down the place." Harry winked at Patsy, who surprised herself by blushing. "I'll put in a good word for you." Harry clapped his hands together with a loud smack, opening them and curling his fingers over the top, whispering into the center. "All good things come to those who ask," he whispered, releasing his hands. A breeze fluttered over the heads of the other magicals, turning into moths that landed neatly on Uncle Petie's shoulder. He leaned over and listened, even as the moths broke apart into soft, cream-colored motes, bouncing in the light. Uncle Petie smiled, twisting the end of his moustache, his fingernails painted a sparkling black.

"I'm not sure you need to go to that much trouble." Patsy nervously patted the pockets of her comfort stretch jeans searching for a stray M&M and let out a sigh at finding nothing. "Of all the times."

"Okay everybody, gather round in a tighter circle." Uncle Petie was waving in different directions at the different pockets of magicals whispering to each other, worried looks on their faces.

Lois was standing next to him doing her best to look calm while waving at Patsy to come join her. "Over here," she whispered loudly as if no one else could hear her.

"Excuse me." Patsy nodded at Harry, demurely pointing at Lois, wondering why she was bothering to explain at all. Harry took a deep bow, particularly for a Gnome and stood up straight, a hand on his chest, smiling. "Perhaps after the meeting you'll let me make you something from the kitchen. I have a real talent for it, you know. A little coconut cream pie?"

Patsy opened her mouth to say something but was interrupted. "Dessert is her love language," said Lois, grabbing Patsy's hand and tugging at her arm, pulling her into motion.

Patsy sputtered with indignation, her cheeks turning red again and tried to smile back at Harry, even as she was quickly walking behind Lois, changing momentarily to a frown. She settled on the smile and chose to deliver just a handful of marble-sized fireballs to dance around Lois' feet.

Lois let out an exasperated yelp, stomping out the rest. She pulled Patsy closer and hissed, "I was helping, and you know it. You're not the fastest at getting things moving in the romance category."

"But I'm a Witch and he's a Gnome."

Lois rolled her eyes and opened her purse, pulling out a worn bag of peanut M&M's. "My emergency stash just for you. Take these. Who cares if you're different? Find out if he's kind. We already know he has a job and can cook. He's two thirds of the way home. Ask me later about the very last third."

Patsy's mouth dropped open, but no sound came out. She looked back at Harry who gave her a smile and a short wave before making his way through the throng and disappearing into the kitchen. She shrugged and watched him go, turning in time to see Uncle Petie raise his arm and twist his hand with a flourish.

The pink elephant suddenly came to life, shaking its large head and lifting her trunk, trumpeting and making the ceiling tiles just overhead vibrate. The miniature pachyderm stomped her front feet and opened her mouth wide, showing the plain paper strips on the interior. A haunting blues melody softly erupted from the papier mâché opening making everyone turn to listen.

The song's notes appeared in the air, bouncing around till they reached Patsy, circling just above her head before fading into nothing.

"Now that's not something you see every day," said Lois. "That Gnome's got game."

"That was Uncle Petie," said Patsy, flustered.

"Sure, but not his idea. Where's the candy? You already finish it?"

Patsy pulled out the weathered bag and stuffed it back in her pocket. "I'm saving room for pie. These can wait."

Lois threw up her hands. "We are living in the weirdest of times."

Uncle Petie snapped his fingers in the air, the elephant returning to its former state and the music ending. Patsy pressed her hand to her chest, wondering about the Gnome, and just a little about the pie.

"Welcome Witches and Wizards, or should I say, Silver Griffin agents. Now, now," said Uncle Petie, waving his arms to quiet the suddenly buzzing crowd. "You're safe to be exactly who you are here. There are no other refugees at the Carousel Lounge at the moment. Too dicey. You have served magicals well and deserve to be protected." Uncle Petie pressed his lips together into a thin line. "At least better than you have been lately," he said, annoyed. He shook his head and smacked his lips together as if he was trying to get rid of a bad taste or an odor and ended with a deep sigh. "So much pain and suffering, though, has turned a few of your brethren into a complication." He smacked the top of his balding head with his hands. "I will let your graceful leader explain. It's not for me to judge. So much pain." He shook his head and stepped back, sweeping his arm to give Lois space.

Lois stepped to the center, pulling Patsy with her. Lois cupped her hand under her chin. "Paulo volumine," she whispered, dropping her hand. "Welcome everyone." The spell carried her voice to each person. "Welcome, fellow agents, really because that's what we all are even to this day." She held up a hand to quiet the few rumblings. "It doesn't matter if we have no infrastructure. That's not what made us an effective organization. It has always been our willingness to do the right thing, even when the darkness threatens to extinguish us, like now."

The sound of paper tearing in the stillness stopped Lois for a moment. She looked over at Patsy, digging through the M&M bag. "What? Oh, sorry. I got nervous for you and needed a little something. Okay, fine!" Patsy pushed half of the bag into her mouth, puffing out her cheeks before stuffing the remaining few back into her pocket. She tried a couple of crunches but one long look from Lois and she settled on letting them slowly melt. "Better that way, anyway," she mumbled through her crowded mouth.

Lois leaned closer and whispered, "You're lucky you're such a good fighter."

"And loyal friend who knows where all your secrets from Ray are buried," muttered Patsy, taking the opportunity for one more good crunch of her teeth. She tried smiling at a nearby Wizard, but the bits of chocolate threatened to spill out and she stopped, choosing to wink at Lois instead, adding a thumbs up.

Lois just stared again, shaking her head before turning

back to the crowd. "Like I was saying, we are still all agents and are still bound by the oath we took when we became agents. The seal that binds us has not been released." She paused, weighing her next words. "But some have chosen to break it." She let the words sink in for the agents. "Broken and angered by circumstance--"

"And who can blame them," yelled out a young Wizard in pale khakis and a brown Jackie Venson t-shirt.

"We can," said Lois, holding up her hand. "We can because we took an oath that we knew could include our death, at any time. None of this is a complete surprise, only the expanse of it. Only that so many of us have paid with our lives. But we don't turn to vengeance and become like those we hunt. We stand in the breach and fight back till we win the day, again. Today, this day, is the new beginning for us. Today is when we start to take back our place in the magical realm." The older Witch raised a fist into the air. "We stop running and we turn to fight as a collective, again. But mark my words, to all who are considering joining the Red Phoenix. You will be on our list as well. Revenge will not go unchecked."

Patsy swallowed the rest of the candy and raised her fist high in the air but only a few others joined her. She narrowed her eyes and turned in a circle, still holding up her arm. "Leonard! You have sixteen years of service. You have been wounded on the job. Hell, you've even been dragged inside a Kilomea cave and almost died. This is where you finally feel defeated? What about you, Emily? You were fresh out of training when all hell broke loose but you said you wanted this your entire life. Did you think this was an office job?"

Lois brushed a tear off her cheek, listening to her oldest friend of a couple hundred years. "Loyal to a fault, no matter what. There's a lot of courage inside that velour. All the fun-sized bars I can wrangle for you, my friend," she muttered, but the spell she had done was still carrying her voice to everyone. A few stood up straighter, listening intently.

"The danger is real and ever present. We have all lost good friends and comrades. But we are the reason magic has been able to exist in this world for thousands of years without the humans losing their shit," said Patsy. "Or the darkness among our kind figuring out how to take over and take away our choices. Come on, agents! Grow up!"

"Aw hell," said the burly Witch from earlier in her low growl. "Fuck it, I'm about ready for another mission, anyway. It's been too long." She turned and faced the crowd. "You heard our leaders. Who's up to taking back what belongs to us and right this system, once and for all? Agnes? Raven?" The Witch thrust her beefy hand into the air, staring down the others, calmly turning in a circle. A Wizard finally came and stood next to her, raising his fist into the air, his back to Patsy and Lois. Slowly but surely, others pushed through the throng of just over a hundred Witches and Wizards and came to the front, silently raising their fists with grim but determined looks on their faces.

Patsy nudged Lois with her elbow. "Look," she whispered, "it's working. You did it!"

Lois put her arm around her friend's shoulders. "We did it, Patsy. And in the end, these are all Silver Griffin agents who passed all the tests to be here today."

"True, but these are special times, and some have failed

us. Badly. A few have even betrayed us. Everyone here has had to flee their homes and their lives with their families. They've seen friends die fiery deaths. Still, they want to serve and that's because we sparked something inside of them."

Lois and Patsy stepped forward and stood among the growing crowd till almost everyone was gathering near the front. "Come on, Bailey," said Patsy, waving at one of the last few. "You know you can't stand being left out."

"Today, we start again," said Lois, smiling, despite all the losses. "We are still the Silver Griffins, and we will make sure everyone respects us and some fear us."

"To a new day!" shouted Patsy, lifting her fist into the air.

"To a new day!" shouted the others, echoing in the bar.

Patsy looked over in time to see Harry standing in the doorway of the kitchen, smiling at her, his fist in the air. In his other hand was a slice of coconut cream pie with a fork carefully laid on the plate.

"To a new day," she muttered. "To all of it, I'm in."

## CHAPTER TWENTY-FIVE

The darkness swirled around Ossonia as she slid between different rooms inside the World in Between, searching for signs of Perrom. The tall, blonde Light Elf pushed her way into a corner, squeezing through and found herself in the far northern part of the Dark Forest. She came as close to the veil separating the worlds as possible, reaching out her hand.

Just beyond her grasp, she could see the ferns swaying in the wind and the tall wildflowers bobbing their heads in time with the sounds of birds singing back and forth to each other. It was all so near.

"I will find you again, Perrom. Don't give up on me."

But there was no sign of him, and she heard the *swish, swish* of the tide that had grown inside the World in Between, threatening magicals. It was getting closer.

She took another quick look around and went to the far corner in what had become a familiar ritual, pushing herself through till she was in another section of the Dark Forest. A family of playful black bear cubs were dancing in a circle, pushing each other to the ground and rolling down a slight incline near a pool of clear water.

*Swish, swish.* Ossonia glanced nervously over her shoulder. The tide was on the prowl searching from room to room. Again. The pursuits had become more frequent and were covering more ground. Rumors were everywhere inside the world among the living and the dead about disappearances. No one could be sure.

*Swish, swish.* The sound was growing louder.

Ossonia took a quick look at the world she once belonged to. "I will again, I swear it." But there was no sign of Perrom. No tiny bits of ribbon tied to tree branches to let her know he had been there. No wildflowers gathered in bunches and left in tree knots. No sign of their initials notched into the bark of trees.

*Swish, swish, swish.* Ossonia got up to run and finally saw something. Nearly hidden by the swaying ferns was a fading simple note painted onto the side of a pine tree. 'I will wait for you. P.'

She looked at the note, studying every detail of it for as long as she dared. "And I will find a way back to you," she shouted, as if her voice could carry into his world and find him. She heard the sound again, and pressed into the wall, falling a few feet before landing in an unfamiliar place.

Just on the other side was an old hotel room but no one in the paintings moved and the lights didn't hang in midair. "I'm not near Oriceran," she said with surprise.

Ossonia moved closer toward the desk on the far wall and read the name on the note pad. "Driskill Hotel, Austin, Texas." Her eyes widened and she turned to get near the window, looking down at the darkened street. "Leira, where are you? Find me, please."

---

Down on the street, a young Witch who was fairly new to town looked up at the windows of the historic hotel and saw the ghostly figure peering out from the eighth-floor room. "Ossonia," gasped Lily Sharpton, a chill running down her back. She hurriedly blew translucent bubbles out of her mouth, fervently whispering into them. She wasn't sure how long she had to get a message to the other side.

The bubbles floated to the eighth floor and popped. "I see you, Ossonia. I'll tell her. Come back here, we'll find you," could be heard just outside the window.

Lily could see Ossonia start and look down, searching out the one still face in the crowd. The throng of students filling Sixth Street flowed around her as she stayed motionless, looking up at the window until Ossonia was gone. "Leira, I have to tell Leira. She'll know what to do. Ossonia has found the hotel room."

# CHAPTER TWENTY-SIX

Leira stood on the crest of the hill of the Gardener's forest just outside of Austin, Texas. The view was of unimpeded rolling grasslands with a herd of Grey Rhebok antelopes grazing nearby, occasionally lifting their heads to sniff the air for predators.

Leira's old friend, Hagan was by her side with Yumfuck sitting quietly on his shoulder. The pair were sharing a Maple Blazer Blunt donut. Both of them had red sprinkles balancing on their round bellies.

"More," squeaked Yumfuck, holding out his paws. Hagan patiently tore off a piece of the fried dough and handed it to the troll. "Hmmm, maple," said Yumfuck, pushing the large piece into his mouth.

The sun was just rising, painting the sky in shades of purple and grey. The warm air felt good across the back of her neck. For just a moment, the Jasper Elf could forget there was anything dangerous out there looking for her. "Not here," she whispered.

"What's that?" asked Hagan, letting out a deep sigh. He took a healthy bite out of the donut and handed the rest to the troll, who happily took it and buried his face in the remains, scattering the rest of the sprinkles. "This is the good life," said Hagan, smiling. "Good God, I'm bored. How does anyone retire? I actually miss listening to a suspect lie to me. I wonder if there's a way the Gardener could help me live out there during the day," he said, pointing in the direction of the southern end of the forest. Miles away was the city of Austin and thousands of people chasing their dreams. Leira felt the warmth inside of her body from being so close to Estelle and her old hometown, and the pain that there was no time to go back and sit at the bar with the regulars. *Not yet.*

"You think the city might want back an old detective?" Hagan waved his hand in frustration, pulling out another donut, carefully wrapped in a napkin. "Aw, never mind. I'm where I'm supposed to be, I guess." He took a deep bite out of the Old Dirty Bastard before tearing off a chocolate chunk for the troll. Chocolate cookie crumbs dropped to his protruding waist to mix in with the red sprinkles. Yumfuck crawled down the front of his shirt to lick them up for his old friend.

Leira looked over at the troll and up at Hagan who was watching the herd begin to run toward the protection of the forest. The hot part of a Texas day was fast approaching, and they had learned to adapt to their new surroundings. Best to seek out cover.

"You two may have gotten a little too comfortable with each other," said Leira, watching the troll finish off the last of the crumbs and climb back onto Hagan's shoulder. Yumfuck leaned back on his paws and let out a satisfied cackle, looking up at the stars that were just beginning to appear. "The best of friends!" he chirped.

"Come on, partner, let's get to it," said Hagan, crossing his arms over his chest. "Show me what you got."

"That's why we're here." Leira knelt to open the backpack at her feet. Inside were a few glass vials full of combinations of herbs, pine sap, roots and mushrooms in different combinations. Each one had a sticker on the outside with a note written in Tess's shaky scrawl.

"How many times have you practiced with Tess so far?"

"Just a few. For an ancient seer who is thought to be dead, she's very busy. It's always more of a feeling lesson than telling me straight out what to do."

"The Gardener must have a lot of faith in both of you to let you test your new seer magic near his forest. I mean, what if fireworks break out?"

"Thanks for the confidence boost." Leira flexed her hands and opened them wide before taking a pinch out of the first vial.

"What's this one for?" Hagan took a step away from Leira's side. "Sorry, old reflex around magic," he said sheepishly. "I like the few strands of hair I have left."

"Is that why you brought your gun with you? Shoot the magic if you have to?"

Hagan chuckled. "I think I just wanted the excuse to have my old piece with me again. Go on, now. Give us a preview before you light up the world."

"This one," said Leira, standing up straight with the

pinch in the palm of her hand. "This is for creating waves of light in the sky."

"Northern lights? Is that what makes those things?"

"Sometimes. But there are so few magicals who practice in partnership with nature, it doesn't happen often. Give me a second."

"Take your time, Leira. You always knew how to trust your gut, even when it was just an instinct that helped us catch a killer. You got this."

Leira blew out air, puffing out her cheeks. She shut her eyes for a moment and opened them again. *A true practitioner needs to see nature to connect on the deepest level.* She could hear Tess's words echo in her head. She held up her hand and let the magic come to her, full of curiosity, winding up her legs and into her chest, circling around her shoulders. *What do you want?* She could feel the question inside the energy.

"Light up the sky." She said it with no expectations it would work, no attachments to how it would work and yet, with a belief that everything was happening in perfect order. Something special was bound to happen.

She kept her breathing steady and felt an expansiveness in her chest. "Anything is possible," she murmured. It was a new feeling that felt like it would roll right off her skin if she focused on it for more than the moment it took to sense it was there.

*Set an intention. First step, then work together. Feel your way into it.*

She said it again. "Light up the sky." The wind picked up immediately, lifting the small grains in her outstretched hand. They coiled in and out of each other, floating in the air and spreading out in every direction, going ever higher.

*Everything is exactly as it's supposed to be. Nature knows what it's doing. Trust everything.* That last part. It was the hardest for Leira. Trust what can't be seen or controlled or forced into submission. Instead, flow with it.

"Do less."

Tess had said those words to her, laughing and rocking back in her chair.

"I think it's working," said Hagan in a hushed voice, his chin tilted up toward the wide, Texas sky. The troll stood up on his shoulder and stretched his paws over his head. "I love magic," he shouted to the stars.

Leira opened her arms wide and felt the different energies mingling, coming in from every quarter. All of nature wanted to weigh in and be a part of the magic. Leira's own energy was a small piece of it, wrapping around and blending in without insisting on anything.

The night sky slowly became illuminated with deep greens and blues that appeared back lit, sparkling in an endless stream. She watched in awe, stretching out her arms and wanting to run across the field underneath the light. The colors spread out, undulating and weaving back and forth.

"Step two," said Leira. "Time to work with the magic and make requests." She felt the open spaces, making sure she was settled into them. "Show me a blanket of stars lit up by the lights."

*Feel the balance between expectation and hope. Hold the space.*

Slowly the light curled, sweeping across the sky

creating a blanket with a million small holes with every star peeking through, twinkling in the fabric made of magic.

Tears filled Leira's eyes and she wiped them away, feeling a connection to magic she had never known before this night. "I'm not alone," she whispered, realizing what the ache was that had existed in her for too many years. She kept looking up at the patchwork of light and color above her saying, "I have to run an errand. You guys okay till I get back?"

"We have donuts and a show. We'll be fine. You can even let the little guy spend the night. Rose would love to see him and there's a train set I've been wanting to show him." Hagan and the troll were both still looking up, their mouths hanging open in awe.

"The universe is an endless marvel," said Yumfuck. "Not to be missed."

"Well said, little fellow." Hagan let out a sigh. "Get going, Leira and we'll be fine. Well done, old partner. You continue to surprise me."

"Enjoy the donuts," said Leira, pulling the familiar pink box out of her backpack and leaving it on the ground. She opened a portal to the kitchen at home and saw Correk leaning into the pantry. He turned around in time to see the lights glowing behind her, the stars twinkling across the horizon.

Leira stepped through and let the portal close behind her, crossing the short distance in a run to throw her weight against him, wrapping her arms around his back and leaning her head on his chest.

"What's this?" Correk kissed the top of her head. "Did

something happen? The troll was smiling and waving when the portal closed. Hagan was upright with a donut in his hand. Is it something else?"

"I felt it," she said, her cheek pressed hard against his soft, blue cotton t-shirt, stretched tight over his chest. "The connection to everything, I felt it. I had no idea."

Correk put his arms around her, squeezing tight.

"It's not something you seek. It's something you just allow, or ask for, or take in. I'm not sure there are words." Leira took a step back, leaning the palms of her hands against his chest. "I have always felt alone to some degree."

Correk's eyes widened only slightly, and he said nothing, just listening to her.

"I mean, you came along, and Yumfuck and so much of it went away. But it was still there playing in the background that I could be alone again. I mean, look at what we do for a living. I never let go of the idea that I could be alone again, and it made it hard to really feel the connection to you." She tapped his chest, her eyes shining with tears again. "I had no idea what I was missing." She gently laid her head on his chest and Correk placed a hand on the top of her head, pressing her closer.

"No matter what ever happens, you and I will be connected forever, Leira Berens. Nothing can separate us. Not time, not even death. I would find you again, and again, and again." He kissed the top of her head again.

"This is what it means to love someone. The feeling of being connected on some other level, completely and without trying to control it." She could feel Correk's heartbeat, steady and strong, underneath her cheek.

"Welcome to the party, Leira."

"I will love you forever." She felt him relax and his heart rate slow down for the first time since the battle. "And I want to stay here forever, with you. There's so much we have left to do with each other."

"Thank you," he whispered. "You finally get it."

"Yeah, I actually think I do."

## CHAPTER TWENTY-SEVEN

Louie opened a portal near Leira and Correk's brownstone in a back alley just down the street. The sword was in its sheath, strapped to his back and humming audibly. It had been nudging him all week to get this done. Go see Leira. But he had waited, trying to straighten out things with Ava.

Besides he needed to be prepared before approaching the bounty hunter or her mate. Louie had too much history with them, some of it dark, to just show up.

He knew he had other business to get to before he could knock on their door even if the sword didn't exactly agree.

*Tell Leira. Make her listen.* "I will, I told you I will. Calm down." *Something evil is invading the magic realm.* "Yes, you said that. I can feel it too. But not so big on filling in the blanks, are you? We need to be professional about this."

He needed more information and all of his connections at the Dark Market had failed him. None of the thieves and con artists knew anything at all. None of the arms dealers knew of anything and turned him away.

That was its own kind of bad sign.

The dark web was quiet too. Too quiet. There was the usual trafficking of any kind of goods or services. There were also too many still looking for Silver Griffin agents' locations and then the bidding took place on the other side to take out certain agents. Old grudges that demanded to be addressed.

But nothing that addressed the trouble he felt roiling across his back.

The sword chimed in again with its dire predictions. *The rules are being broken.* Something was interfering with the basic elemental rules of magic and the threat was only growing.

That was the one that was getting to him the most. Every time the sword said it, he felt his stomach tie into knots and the same sensation creep across his neck.

The spark of humanity inside of him, mixed with the wizardry he inherited from his mother, was letting him feel the kink in the patchwork of magic that was everywhere, all at once, but often ignored.

"Someone is fucking with it," he whispered, not for the first time. But he didn't have much more than that to tell Leira, and it sounded a little overdone, especially for him. He was getting down to his last sources who were good for inside dirt. The Willens.

Louie laid out the pile of old tin and brass artifacts as instructed by an old Willen named Spinster that hung around the tables at the market. Louie regularly fed her, even giving her the occasional small trinket that just wasn't selling. Most merchants ignored her, or worse, and were repaid with evening raids when the market was quiet. Willens would come in, unseen and steal bits and pieces from the offending parties and leave without a trace.

Louie was the same kind of operator and knew immediately who was behind it. He said nothing to no one. He was no snitch, especially in a market where a tattler was the lowest form of life and generally didn't live long enough to rat someone out again.

Spinster was more than happy to tell him about the rumors she had heard about the Willens searching for information in the other world about a new menace. Something insidious, said the old Willen. Something so deadly even the Willens were making plans to leave for Oriceran, at least for a little while, if necessary.

Spinster had rubbed her whiskers and told him to find the alley a block away from the bounty hunter who's a Jasper Elf, surprising Louie. The Willens had made a trade with a nearby troll and were known to hang out in the area, waiting for further instructions or more payment.

"Yumfuck Tiberius Troll," said Louie, crouching by an old entrance to an abandoned underground tunnel. X235 was in raised metal letters on the top, just like Spinster told him. "A Willen address."

He knelt down on one knee and placed the loot near the entrance, knocking three times loudly, pausing and knocking three times again.

The pieces were nearly worthless to him. All of the magical energy inside of them had mostly drained away.

But the Willens would find it a worthwhile trade for the shine and glitter. "Bonus points, most of this can hold stuff." Louie arranged the pieces, making as much noise as possible and then sat back on the ground and waited.

It wasn't too long before the cover lifted and a paw with long, slender claws reached out of the opening to grab a small brass bowl with etchings around the rim. Louie let that one go, giving the Willen a sample.

The paw emerged again, reaching for the next closest item, a tin box painted on the side. But this time, he scooched it a little further away, watching the paw stretch a little further.

Louie leaned closer and whispered, "First we make a trade. Then all of it is yours." The paw quickly retracted, and Louie sat back, patiently waiting. Good negotiations were as much about patience and staying calm as anything else. He had a little time and he needed this to go well. There was no one left to ask.

He could hear the hushed, breathy voices of several Willens, some of them scratching the walls with frustration or to make calculations. The sword pressed against his back, the vibrations intensifying, making it harder for him to sit still. *Find Leira and tell her.*

"Message received," he muttered.

Finally, the lid lifted and was flipped to one side. Three large grey Willens in matching orange construction vests with shiny reflection tape climbed out, one after the other, furtively looking around for signs of trouble. The biggest one was wearing worn leather sneakers with a hole in the toe where a claw poked out.

They looked at Louie and the sword on his back and stayed close to the opening, glancing back down at the tunnel and relative safety. No one was willing to come closer.

"Spinster sent me. She said you could be useful for the right price. All this can be yours for a little information." He swept his hand over the pile, game show style.

"Spinster," hissed the smallest of the Willens. "She's good people."

"She said to tell you that Nala misses you and she knows you took her best silver spoons." Louie arched a brow and crossed his arms. Spinster had sworn this would work.

"Yeah, that's Spinster. I told you not to fleece her." The largest Willen, who was resting on his haunches in the middle gave a loud tsk but nudged the Willen in front of him. "Go on Puzzles. Test the goods."

"Don't push me, Reginald. I don't like being rushed." Puzzles reached out to squeeze the tin box, making clicking noises against his teeth, his whiskers shivering. "Uh huh, uh huh, hmmmm," he muttered, seemingly satisfied, smacking his lips together and licking his sharp front teeth.

Reginald got up and waited for Puzzles to get out of the way, settling himself closer to Louie and the pile of metal objects. "What do you want to know?"

"What did Yumfuck ask you to do?"

Reginald dropped the nickel bracelet, but Louie saw him palm a small brass bowl, slipping it quickly into the folds of his skin. Louie tilted his head and let the sword slip off his shoulder and swing around, down into his lap. "I need to know so I can tell Leira Berens."

"We owe Yumfuck the intel first."

"You owe whoever is currently paying you. That would be me."

Reginald laughed a high-pitched squeal, patting his orange vest. "You understand the ways of the Willens. You have a little of us in you too, don't you?" The Willen leaned closer, studying Louie's eyes.

Louie wrinkled his forehead, patiently waiting. "Always possible. I'm a kind of mutt." He pressed down on the sword in his lap. The vibrations were growing ever stronger. "Tell me what Yumfuck wanted you to do. Then tell me what you found."

"That will take two payments," said Reginald, eyeing the sword.

"The sword? You don't want this. It's very particular about its owners. Go on, put your hand closer, but a warning, don't touch it."

Reginald looked at him from the side, frowning, but he slowly reached out a paw, inching toward the sword. He stopped abruptly inches from the metal. "It's blazing hot! How are you keeping it in your lap?"

The other Willens drew closer, putting out a paw and found the same results.

"I told you. Very particular. But I have more loot with me. We can make a trade," said Louie, pulling out the cloth bag that had been sitting behind his bag and shaking it. The items inside clanked together, satisfying the Willens. Louie put the bag back out of sight. "If what you have is worth it."

Reginald sat back, licking his paws, delighted. "Oh, it's worth it. Yumfuck asked us to look for tears between this world and the World in Between. Tears that don't ever close."

Reginald got the response he was hoping for as Louie leaned back, the color draining from his face.

"Did you-- did you find any?" The words came out haltingly.

"We found a few, which is too many. They're all protected by something that we dare not cross or examine too closely. You can hear through the tears. Horrible sounds. Screaming and moaning." Reginald's entire body shook, letting the hidden loot he was carrying with him clang together creating a kind of body chimes.

"Okay, a deal's a deal. This pile of loot is all yours," said Louie, pushing the initial pile he set up toward the Willens. They quickly divided the items amongst themselves with relatively little arguing and only a few nips and scratches. In no time, all of it had disappeared into the folds of their skin.

"What about the rest of it?

"What more do you have for me? It has to be something useful I can take to Leira."

The Willen rubbed his chin, tilting his head and eyeing Louie. "We want the same things, you know. This is a threat to all of us."

"Tell him," said Puzzles. "Tell him everything. He'll pay us."

Louie pulled the bag around and opened the sack, digging around till he found the tiara made of nickel with shiny glass jewels embedded in it. "Here, take this as a down payment and sign of good will."

Puzzles snatched at it, planting it on his head before Reginald could stop him.

Reginald rolled his eyes, frustrated. "Fine, I'll tell you, but you won't like it. He leaned closer to Louie and hissed, "There is now more than one Dark Mist. Leira thinks she is fighting one great blob that seeks her out. Doesn't she wonder how it keeps finding her in so many different places? It's subdivided itself and branching out. Like an octopus it can grow new tentacles, only these arms stay in touch."

Louie froze, staring at the Willens like he had to have heard them wrong.

"Say something, dude. We don't know how to resuscitate your fleshy kind."

"Yeah, we might poke a hole in something you need."

"Scratch him and see if he jumps."

Louie stood quickly before the Willens could reach him, slinging the sword onto his back. He leaned down for the bag and tossed it close to Reginald. "Here, take all of it. You've more than earned it." His eyes were still wide and he stumbled back a few steps, almost tripping. He turned and began running in the direction of the brownstone, willing himself to go faster.

"Say hello to Spinster for us," yelled Puzzles as Reginald dumped out the contents of the bag and they once again divided up the loot.

"The Dark Mist is building an army," said Louie, trying to catch his breath and wondering if he should stop and throw up in the nearest trash can.

*Tell Leira now.* The sword was warming against his back. "Yeah, I get it now. Tell her as fast as possible. Soon, the Dark Mist will be everywhere and there will be no place left to hide."

## CHAPTER TWENTY-EIGHT

Leira stood at the end of the paved road just outside of Cozad, Nebraska where the blacktop branched off into three dirt roads surrounded by old mossycup oak trees. Tess was beside her in a loose-fitting dress and long apron tied at the back. The old seer bounced on her toes, suddenly agile, with her hands by her sides and a determined scowl on her face.

"You were right to make Turner Underwood find me. Ignore his protests. If all I'm good for anymore is occasional vague sentiments, then it's time I passed to the other side. My usefulness will have been spent." Tess balled her hands into fists, flexing her fingers and splaying them back out again.

"I want to believe you."

"Well, belief may have to come later. You're here and that's most of the battle. You're willing." Tess's face was turned toward the empty road where it split into the different directions. "Trust me now with everything you have and don't let go. This is necessary. I need to show you something so you can sleep at night."

Leira let out the breath she was holding. Tess knew her far too well. Ever since Louie had burst into their back door yelling throughout the house, insisting they listen, Leira had not been able to sleep through the night. *Was that only a few days ago?*

"The Dark Mist has split into different sections, all of them operating as one," she muttered.

Yumfuck had grown to his full height in the front hall, roaring at full volume in shock and anger making the small chandelier by the stairs sway violently.

Only Correk had stood by quietly, taking it all in and measuring his words. "Find Tess," he said, once everyone had calmed down enough to hear him. "Find Tess and ask her what to do."

This was how Leira had ended up standing in the middle of nowhere in Nebraska. "I'm at a literal crossroads trying to use a magical Ouija board to call up hell."

Tess gave a dark laugh. "You have a firm grasp of the situation. We will conjure the Dark Mist to come out and play. You *need* to see something. There is no darkness that can ultimately defeat light. The question really is whether or not there's enough light."

"Are you saying I possess enough light? Won't that kill me?"

"No and yes if you go it alone, in that order."

"Comforting." Leira shifted her weight. She was wearing her favorite Hoka running shoes for no real reason. Leira knew she would never leave Tess standing there unprotected.

"I'm never unprotected, dear. I am one with Nature and always looked after by everything that grows. Everything that has a beating heart that hasn't been poisoned by a darkened sentient mind knows my name."

"How do you always know what I'm thinking?"

"I just answered that question. Listen closely and maintain your connection with all of Nature, with a capital N. Allow everything and anything that has even the smallest amount of light to help you. I will do the same. We will shine a light so bright, the Dark Mist will ooze over itself trying to get to us. And then, the real fun begins."

"Great, good times."

"Okay, ready?" But Tess didn't wait for a response. Her body began to emanate light as the trees around them trembled. Leira felt her belly lurch with the surge of energy suddenly pouring into the cavity of her chest. Her eyes started to glow and her skin warmed, giving off its own light. "This is new," she muttered. "Tess, can I handle this much light?"

"Trust me," shouted Tess over the rumble that was erupting deep in the earth. Everything around them was conspiring to join forces and help share some of their light.

It wasn't long before Leira smelled the oily brine and knew the Dark Mist, or at least some piece of it, was close. Tess had said she knew there was a tear nearby but never revealed how she sensed it.

"Maybe that's tomorrow's lesson. If there's a tomorrow." Leira felt a hum come up through the ground and into her feet.

"Open yourself up and stop operating from fear. That doubt? It's fear because you can't step forward and be in control. Let your strength come from a sense that all is well with the world, and you are one piece of a massive, loving puzzle. The darkness doesn't know what to do with that urge. It can either rise to meet the feeling or is compelled to leave." Tess was now glowing so brightly only an outline of her small frame was visible.

Leira gave in to the sense of peace and calm rising inside of her, despite the gooey mist growing closer. "I can do this."

The Dark Mist slid easily over the paved road, picking up pebbles and leaves, burying them in the ooze. The tops of heads and hands were clawing the air, rising out of the thick, gelatinous monster that was rolling toward Leira and Tess.

For one moment, Leira felt herself slip, wondering if she was betraying her promise to Correk to at least try to stay alive. But just as she could feel the wonder and energy of nature pause to question whether or not she was willing to trust and let go of control, she felt Tess's small, bony hand suddenly rest heavily on her shoulder. The warmth of her compassion and the firmness of her resolve passed as energy into Leira's bones and muscles, infusing Leira with the same feeling of connection she had experienced before.

It was intoxicating.

"Don't let your usual senses dictate how things have to turn out. Go inward and trust, trust, trust."

"Trust everything." Leira held out her hand for Tess and wrapped her fingers gently around the ancient seer's hand. It gave her just enough conviction to finally let go.

The sweep of the Dark Mist rolled within feet of the pair and suddenly stopped, rising up in a black wall of thick liquid containing too many dead magicals tossing about inside its depths. The darkness shimmered and became smooth as glass till Leira could see her own reflection bubbling on its surface.

But for once, she stood firm and didn't fight back, letting the energy that was passing through her come to a collective decision to hold out the light as an offering and not a rebuke. Let the Dark Mist decide what it wanted to do next.

The blaze of light intensified, spreading out over the three roads and up into the trees. Birds scattered, taking to the skies in a loud rush, telling other creatures far afield to join in the connection.

"Keep hold," said Tess.

The Dark Mist began to crest at the top of the wave that stood nearly ten feet tall. The rest of the Dark Mist stretched out behind it for a hundred yards, leaking into this world from a tear in the roots of a tall tree.

*Whatever happens, we are alright.* Leira repeated the words over and over again, letting the warmth of the connection pass through her.

Bits and pieces at the top of the wave began to break apart, falling backward onto itself, thinning out the tide. Leira watched in amazement as the Dark Mist lost some of its shape and size.

It wasn't long before the Dark Mist began to roll back toward where it came into the side of the living leaving a slimy, dark stain coated in bits of dirt. Desperate hands and faces wide open in despair and horror leaned toward Leira and Tess throughout the entire retreat.

The light gradually dimmed, and a quiet came back to

the fields that caught Leira off guard. Everything was still as if all of nature were waiting to see if there would be a second request to come together.

Tess let go of Leira's hand and brushed strands of her white hair off her face, pinching the bridge of her nose. "The Dark Mist made a decision. Its plans, its designs to control everything were more important. So be it."

"It's not defeated, is it?"

Tess chuckled, ending in a low hum. "No, not at all. It has merely learned there may be limits and it's probably rethinking things."

"That can't be good."

"My dear, stop thinking in terms of good or bad. Nature only knows consequences. We take everything so personally that we want to come back at who or what we perceive as enemies, with weapons and anger." Tess smiled, turning her face up toward the sun that was dappling the roadway. "Weapons are useless against this creature and will only feed its resolve. Fear will do the same. We cannot be just another weapon if we are to change the consequences of this venture. Instead, think of our combined energy as an opportunity. At this level of gamesmanship, only opportunity has a chance at success."

"If our opportunity doesn't tear the Dark Mist's dead limbs apart, how do we get rid of it, once and for all?"

"We may never do that, who knows? But perhaps the creature will do that for us. Bang against our energy over and over again, losing bits and pieces till it wears itself out."

Leira felt the remnants of the connection to nature's power clinging to her, leaving behind traces. She looked up surprised, a crooked smile spreading across her face. "Our real power lies in our ability to come together and make space for everything."

Tess clapped her hands together. "You are learning quickly, Leira Berens. Fear not, for fear is the true enemy. Now, while we're here, let's practice a little more magic. I happened to bring just a few potions with me."

## CHAPTER TWENTY-NINE

The old water tower in Chicago was slowly being rebuilt and repaired. The outside of the building was completed along with new windows enhanced by magic to show a finished interior. But inside, the lobby bore burn marks from fireballs and gashes in the wall, along with blood spatter everywhere.

Only the underground vault had been cleared of debris and fallen agents or enemies.

"It's time," said Lois, standing in the remains of the old lobby. The black, patent leather purse dangled from her wrist.

Only the stairs down to the vault had been completely repaired.

"But why here?" asked Patsy, sucking on a hard butterscotch candy. "Why make everyone deal with all the memories and the grief every day they come here?"

Lois started down the stairs, checking the new wards as she passed through each one. The safeguards had been reinforced with spells from older books checked out of the

Light Elves' library on Oriceran. The Gnomes had personally delivered them with a request from Queen Saria to use them as long as needed. A green leafy vine from her crown was pressed into one of the books. 'For good luck,' was written on the bottom of the note.

"That's precisely the reason. If we don't confront what happened here it will haunt each of us, one way or another. Pain has to be given a voice if we are all to heal and get on with things."

"Even if the voice is full of rage and loud and messy?"

"In all its forms and we will each take turns listening. Follow me down to the new vault. I want to hold a ceremony with all of us gathered for our new start. It's almost time."

Lois held out her hand for her old friend and they walked down the rest of the steps together, passing through the different charmed barriers.

Each ward was designed to be more restrictive than the one before, starting with a blue flame that could not be put out once it engulfed the trespasser. But Lois was the first registrant of the new interior and the ward instantly recognized her. The next ward had razor sharp metal edges that would protrude and cut through any shield. The next howled in a way that caused an intruder's brain matter to turn to jelly. On down the stairs till the fifteenth ward was passed.

Patsy was right next to Lois, marveling at the pleasant scent of a hundred different fern varieties. "I like the new signature scent," said Patsy, biting down hard on the candy and splintering it into pieces.

"Ferns have existed in the same static state since long

before we came into the picture, surviving all kinds of cataclysmic events. The fractal of the fern is already imprinted in our minds from the beginning of magical existence. The scent will heal our bodies and minds and even enhance our ability to smell danger." What Lois didn't add was the idea had come from Tess, the old seer, but her continued existence was the deepest of secrets.

"Ready?" They entered the first chamber that was redone with a large, raised cement bowl full of water. "Come on in, the water's fine."

Patsy snorted and stepped into the water, instantly spinning around, finding herself in a flash standing in a glass-enclosed room that overlooked the new vault floor. Lois wasn't far behind her, the purse still securely on her arm. Patsy patted her cardigan for even a drop of water, but there was nothing. "Amazing," she whispered.

Lois went to the window and looked down at the hundreds of expectant faces looking back at her. She swallowed hard, her throat aching from relief and pain in even measures. "Courage," she muttered. Patsy joined her, pressing a hand against the glass. "They still want to serve, after everything. I don't know what to say. Each one has a family and yet, they showed up for work today."

Lois pressed her lips together, blinking her eyes. "It's an honor to be a Silver Griffin agent today, Patsy. You can lead the way."

"And so it is." Patsy blew into the rubber tubing jutting out from one of the walls. The magical components of her DNA spread out across the wall, creating a door that swiftly opened with a glittering five hanging in the air that immediately began counting down. Patsy quickly stepped through before it reached zero, erasing the door. She'd already been warned that there were only three tries per day and then she would have to wait. No one else could jump in behind her without their DNA being checked first. Those who tried would be instantly turned to ash.

Lois went next, blowing into the tube and swiftly making her way onto the metal stairs, quickly following Patsy down to the main floor that stretched on for miles, courtesy of Turner Underwood. His inaugural gift to the Silver Griffins.

Patsy went and joined the others, stopping to pat the new oversized candy machine before taking her place in the front. Her first contribution to the new headquarters.

Lois stepped onto the platform in front of them and held out her hands, the purse dangling from her wrist. "Welcome agents to our new home. Today, we begin anew. Let the world know that we still exist, and we are no longer running from, but going toward any that choose to twist magic into something evil. Our numbers are growing with new recruits applying every day." She paused, looking out over the faces of so many agents she recognized and some she called friends. "We will always remember those who have fallen in service to all of magic and we will continue with the same devotion to duty in their names. You each have your new assignments and for the time being every new case will be handled by at least two agents. No one travels alone. We are a strong, connected community and we will fight as one."

She looked back over her shoulder at the stairs and the glass entryway. She turned back and held out the purse. "All of the wards have been changed and are now tied to each of our magical traces. That is because some Silver Griffins have decided there has to be another way and have taken it upon themselves to seek revenge. They are calling themselves the Red Phoenix." A murmur rose from pockets in the crowd but quickly stopped. "Someday, you may be tasked with bringing in one of your former colleagues. Do it with care and with compassion but fulfill your duty none the less. No one who has shed the bond of the Silver Griffins will pass through our doors and down those stairs. No one."

Lois nodded at Patsy who turned around and said, "Reveal to me, all that is unseen, all that is mine." One by one the new shelves appeared, stretching back further and further. Different sized spaces and cubbies. Large metal doors appeared on distant walls leading to other areas specially made for creatures that needed a new home.

"Now, let us begin again." Lois snapped open the purse, pulling the sides wide and whispered into the contents deep inside, "Welcome home." She set the purse down on the front of the platform and stood back, watching in awe at the release of so much magic.

Artifacts of every variety emerged. Trumpets that played magical tunes to entrance and capture. Bottles that could ensnare someone's essence. Lipstick to change a face. The list went on and on as each item popped out and then flew to its appropriate new spot, safely secure once again.

Agents cheered and clapped their hands, watching the parade of magical items fly over their heads or spread out to find its spot to the right or the left.

"Once this phase is complete, creatures will be brought here to live in safety and comfort and we will once again, protect this area with everything we've got for as long as we can, and then some." Lois held up her arms, her fingers spread wide. "Let everyone who doubted us know that we not only survive, we thrive and we are out there guarding the magical world, once again."

A loud hurrah went up from the gathered agents. "Now, back to work," said Lois, swallowing hard. *Stay safe, all of you.* She smiled and turned to head for the stairs, quickly brushing a tear off her cheek.

# CHAPTER THIRTY

Uncle Felix was holding a large black umbrella, standing on the hillside, looking back at the house. Rain was pelting the dome of the umbrella. Thunder was cracking over his head and lightning was zigzagging across the sky.

No matter. Lightning had already struck the umbrella, electricity traveling swiftly down the metal shaft and into his hand giving him a pleasurable pulse of energy. It was one of his favorite pastimes in any thunderstorm. He'd been doing it since he was a child.

"It's time for a change," he yelled at the storm. "My dear niece has had her chance and look at us. Ariana wants to play nice. Where has that ever gotten this family?" His face was twisted in anger and frustration. "Soon, dear Ariana, you will see what happens when you can't listen to reason." He started walking back toward the house just as lightning lit up the sky again and he felt the hum through the umbrella. "A good sign," He muttered. "Plans are already in motion. My day is near. I'll be sorry to see you go." His lips curled into a smile.

---

Ariana watched her uncle from an upstairs window. She saw him arch his back and yell at the sky, letting the raindrops hit his face. "You are up to something, you ancient bastard. Not to worry. I have a few tricks left and allies you never dreamed of, but you will come to know them. Soon enough, everyone will."

# THE STORY CONTINUES

Leira's story continues with book fourteen, *Power of Magic*, available at Amazon.

Claim your copy today!

Get sneak peeks, exclusive giveaways, behind the scenes content, and more. PLUS you'll be notified of special **one day only fan pricing** on new releases.

Sign up today to get free stories.

Visit: https://marthacarr.com/read-free-stories/

## AUTHOR NOTES - MARTHA CARR

### DECEMBER 29, 2023

At last, another new Leira book is out. More troll! More troll! It's amazing how fast time goes by and other series call to me, but even I missed finding out what Yumfuck does next or how Leira is growing into her power.

I hope this book, and a couple more new ones, satisfies the craving, for now.

Meanwhile, I'm headed out to Costa Rica to ring in the New Year with four nights of ayahuasca and a lot of shamans. It's my second trip (pun intended) and I figured this will really get the year started off with a bang. Imagine the story ideas I will bring back home.

My first time visiting Rythmia, (a bougie resort because come on, if you're gonna do it, go to the comfy place), was only a year ago and the clarity it brought me helped me change a lot of things. The biggest one is probably, I stopped working so, so much and found a good man named, Mike. (Different Mike and no, I don't know why I keep finding the good Mikes of the world.)

My Mike is a rare find who has a sense of humor and

sings to me out of the blue, often grabbing me for a quick twirl. He even cooks occasionally. I'm the clean up crew. Even better, he makes me laugh all the time.

The key change was I find it easier to be grateful for what is, and I have stopped looking so much for those corners of perfection. I can allow myself to be happy without first taking a general inventory.

And for those of you who read all the author notes, I won the bet with Stephen Campbell who paid up and sent me a signed dollar bill. The bet was a dollar and if Steve wrote another book first, he won. If I managed to get three dates with the same person, I won. It only took me four years to win. Okay, okay, I still won. I'm framing it for posterity.

I also took off all that quarantine weight, at last! Side note, Mike asked me out before I lost most of the weight and told me I was beautiful, so he's a real keeper. But the weight had to go. I wasn't happy with it. I showed up at a weight-lifting class that meets at 6:30 in the morning and just did my best. Sure, after the first class I thought I had sprained the back of my arm. Nope. Apparently, that was a muscle I don't use very often and was protesting at first. But it got better.

I also went back to running, an old love of mine. It took forever to finally conquer running one mile without stopping, but eventually I got there. Now, I'm signed up for the Chicago Marathon this October and it's right when I turn 65. Kind of a cool way to celebrate.

I've also cleaned out every closet and cupboard and drawer in this house. It always bothered me that this is a fairly large house and even though only one person lived here, every drawer and closet was packed. Plus, I never opened most of those drawers. Time for a purge.

Twelve bags to Goodwill later, I could actually see what I have and use all of it. Someone else can benefit from that salad spinner.

Last big thing that changed was I finally learned how to ask for help. I changed the bar from, if I can do it myself, I will – to – let's just ask for help and not do everything, especially if it's hard or scary. Like going to those every six month screenings for cancer that I will have to do for the rest of my life. I was doing all of that alone. Now, Mike travels with me.

Back to that trip to Rythmia. They ask you to come up with an intention for what you hope to learn or heal during the trip. After this past year, mine is to let go of all the old stories I have carried around forever. Labels like girl who's had cancer five times. I can let that go. Or another is I need to work hard to prove something to someone, somewhere. I'm pretty sure no one cares. Maybe there's an easier way. I mean, does it have to be hard? That's the other part of my intention. Let's look for the fun way to do something. It's out there if I look for it.

Let me know your intentions for 2024 and what you hope to leave behind in your personal rearview mirror. So grateful all of you are on this ride with me. Onward! More adventures to follow.

## AUTHOR NOTES - MICHAEL ANDERLE

### JANUARY 4, 2024

Hello, dear friends and fellow travelers on this journey we call life thank you for not only reading this book – but joining Martha and I here in the back!

As you've likely noticed, I often share reflections in these notes that stem from the worlds I create. However, today I'd like to take a step back and reflect on something a bit closer to home—my real life, the day-to-day Michael Anderle that isn't surrounded by the fantastical. You know, the guy who puts his pants on one leg at a time.

(Yes, I'm stupid enough to have tried jumping into them – let's not go there.)

**A Year Embracing 'Simplicity'**

This year, I've chosen to embrace 'Simplicity' as a theme instead of a New Years Resolution.

It's more than just a word; it's a philosophy that will be infiltrating every aspect of my life. You see, there's a profound tranquility I've found in minimalism—keeping things clean not only in my physical surroundings but also within my mental space. An uncluttered desk leads to an uncluttered mind, and an organized home paves the way for an organized thought process.

It's a work in process – don't look at my office at the moment – just saying.

Martha, my incredible collaborator, shared a nugget of wisdom that resonated deeply with my journey towards simplicity: "The key change was I find it easier to be grateful for what is, and I have stopped looking so much for those corners of perfection. I can allow myself to be happy without first taking a general inventory." This sentiment can become an additional meditation for me, reinforcing the notion that happiness isn't contingent upon perfection.

**Living in the Present**

Simplicity (so far – it's only one week) has transformed my approach to life.

I've learned to appreciate the here and now and to find contentment in the moment. It's a cup of tea savored in silence, the laughter of friends that isn't rushed, and the sunset viewed without the urge to capture it for anyone else's eyes but my own.

And stories re-read to spend time with those characters one more time.

Simplicity has also meant letting go of the endless pursuit of 'more'—more gadgets, more commitments, more of everything—and instead, investing in quality, not quantity. I've discovered that a few well-loved items bring far greater joy than a multitude of possessions that serve little purpose. It's only taken me 56 years.

I learn…*slow*.

**Gratitude as a Foundation**

## AUTHOR NOTES - MICHAEL ANDERLE

Martha's approach to gratitude is an additional way to think and ground me in the face of life's inevitable chaos. It's a reminder to be thankful for the small victories—a tidy room, a well-made meal, a day without distractions. This gratefulness extends beyond the tangibles; it's an appreciation for the people around me, the health I enjoy, and the simple freedom to live authentically.

As I continue to navigate this year of 'Simplicity,' I do so with a heart full of gratitude and a mind which hopefully will be liberated by the release of unnecessary complexities. It's a beautiful way to live, and I hope to carry this theme with me as the years unfold, in writing and in life.

Thank you for indulging me in these personal musings. May you find your own theme that brings peace and fulfillment into your world for this year.

Until our next story together,
Michael Anderle

P.S. If you're curious about following me for occasional musings, coupons and thoughts – Join me here: https://michael.beehiiv.com/

BOOKS BY MARTHA CARR

THE LEIRA CHRONICLES
CASE FILES OF AN URBAN WITCH
THE EVERMORES CHRONICLES
CHRONICLES OF WINLAND UNDERWOOD
SOUL STONE MAGE
THE KACY CHRONICLES
MIDWEST MAGIC CHRONICLES
THE FAIRHAVEN CHRONICLES
DIARY OF A DARK MONSTER
I FEAR NO EVIL
THE DANIEL CODEX SERIES
SCHOOL OF NECESSARY MAGIC
SCHOOL OF NECESSARY MAGIC: RAINE CAMPBELL
ALISON BROWNSTONE
FEDERAL AGENTS OF MAGIC
SCIONS OF MAGIC
THE UNBELIEVABLE MR. BROWNSTONE
DWARF BOUNTY HUNTER
ACADEMY OF NECESSARY MAGIC
MAGIC CITY CHRONICLES
ROGUE AGENTS OF MAGIC
WITCH WARRIOR
THE AGENT OPERATIVE
BIG EASY BOUNTY HUNTER

OTHER BOOKS BY JUDITH BERENS

OTHER BOOKS BY MARTHA CARR

JOIN THE ORICERAN UNIVERSE FAN GROUP ON FACEBOOK!

# BOOKS BY MICHAEL ANDERLE

**Sign up for the LMBPN** email list to be notified of new releases and special deals!

http://lmbpn.com/email/

For a complete list of books by Michael Anderle, please visit:

www.lmbpn.com/ma-books/

# CONNECT WITH THE AUTHORS

**Martha Carr Social**
Website:
http://www.marthacarr.com
Facebook:
https://www.facebook.com/groups/MarthaCarrFans/

**Michael Anderle**

Website: http://lmbpn.com

Email List: https://michael.beehiiv.com/

https://www.facebook.com/LMBPNPublishing

https://twitter.com/MichaelAnderle

https://www.instagram.com/lmbpn_publishing/

https://www.bookbub.com/authors/michael-anderle

www.ingramcontent.com/pod-product-compliance
Lightning Source LLC
LaVergne TN
LVHW041906070526
838199LV00051BA/2527